BOSTON NOIR

BOSTON NOIR

EDITED BY DENNIS LEHANE

Published by Akashic Books
©2009 Akashic Books

Series concept by Tim McLoughlin and Johnny Temple
Boston map by Sohrab Habibion

ISBN-13: 978-1-933354-91-0
Library of Congress Control Number: 2009922932
All rights reserved

First printing

Akashic Books
PO Box 1456
New York, NY 10009
info@akashicbooks.com
www.akashicbooks.com

ALSO IN THE AKASHIC NOIR SERIES:

FORTHCOMING:

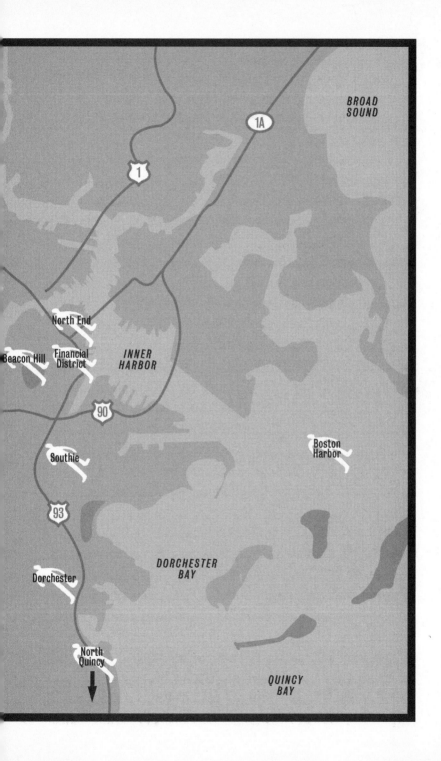

TABLE OF CONTENTS

PART III: VEILS OF DECEIT

INTRODUCTION
TRIBALISM & KNUCKLEHEADS

N o matter what you may hear to the contrary, noir is not a genre defined by fedoras, silver streams of cigarette smoke, vampy femme fatales, huge whitewall tires, mournful jazz playing in the gloomy background, and lots and lots of shadows. Nor is it simply skuzzy people doing skuzzy things to other skuzzy people, a kind of trailer park opera. One *could* argue that what it is, however, is working-class tragedy. Aristotle, when he defined tragedy, mandated that a tragic hero must fall from a great height, but Aristotle never imagined the kind of roadside motels James M. Cain could conjure up or saw the smokestacks rise in the Northern English industrial hell of Ted Lewis's *Get Carter*. In Shakespeare, tragic heroes fall from mountaintops; in noir, they fall from curbs. Tragic heroes die in a blaze of their own ill-advised conflation. Noir heroes die clutching fences or crumpled in trunks or, in the case of poor Eddie Coyle, they simply doze off drunkenly in a car and take one in the back of the head before they have a chance to wake up again. No wise final words, no music swelling on the soundtrack.

Eddie Coyle is a good example here because if there's a more seminal noir novel of the last forty years than *The Friends of Eddie Coyle*, I don't know of it. And more than just being a seminal noir, it's also the quintessential Boston novel. It captures the tribalism of the city, the fatalism of it, and the outsized humor of people who believe God likes a good laugh, usually at your expense. Boston is a city that produces guys—or, in the city's vernacular, knuckleheads—who once stole the replica of a cow that sat in front of a Braintree steak house. The cow weighed what a car weighed, and yet these knuckleheads had the industry to get it onto a pickup truck, drive it back to South Boston, and deposit it in the middle of Broadway. They did this *solely* so they could then call the Boston Police Department and ask them to respond to a "beef going down on Broadway."

In Boston something doesn't simply hurt, it hurts "like a bastid." *Pisser* is a noun that means something funny, but *pissa* is an adjective (and sometimes an adverb) that equates unequivocal greatness, although it's often equivocated with *wicked*, as in, "Big Papi hit a wicked pissa homa against the Yankees. Musta hurt them like a bastid."

So we have our distinct humor and our distinct accent and our distinct vocabulary. All of which—sadly, possibly—is now endangered by progress. Because one can't ignore that Boston has been beset by a new class war of late, one you'll see reflected in the stories herein. It's a war of gentrification. As the city continues to lose its old-school parochialism and overt immigrant tribalism, it's also losing a lot of its character. Whether that's a bad thing or a good thing is up for debate, but what can't be argued is that it is, in fact, happening. South Boston is no longer dominated by buzz cuts and bar brawls; these days, Charlestown's only "code of silence" pertains to failing to tell people about a new restaurant on Warren Street because you don't want to have to start waiting for a table. The Italian tongues of the North End are being phased out by voices questioning why there's no Crate & Barrel beside the Paul Revere House. It's a less violent city now than it ever was, but a beiger one too. I have no doubt the old Boston will rear its head with pride and fury for a long time to come, but I admit to feeling loss when I walk through Kenmore Square these days and see only a kind of soft-rock version of what it used to be. That's the paradox of the new Boston—what's lost has, in many cases, been taken; what's left is what people can't sell. Noir is a genre of loss, of men and women unable to roll with the changing times, so the changing times instead roll over them.

Often a noir hero or antihero doesn't die from being rolled over. But he might prefer he had. The Machine frequently leaves him crushed, attenuated, castrated. No art form that I know of rages against the machine more violently than noir. Hip-hop, arguably, but noir refuses to indulge in hip-hop delusions of grandeur or self-aggrandizement. Noir rages without much hope, certainly without romanticism or wish fulfillment.

But Boston gives noir the strain of humor you never expect, which comes at you from directions you could never predict. The guys who placed that stolen cow in the middle of Broadway would fit perfectly in the pages you're about to read. The journey ranges from a pitch-black discourse on sin in John Dufresne's "The Cross-Eyed Bear" to a haplessly absurd kidnapper in Jim Fusilli's "The Place Where He Belongs," from the deliciously strange relationship between a black divorcée and a white escaped convict in Patricia Powell's "Dark Waters" to Don Lee's chilling meditation on questions of identity and self in "The Oriental Hair Poets," to a carload of knucklehead armed robbers tooling around North Quincy in Russ Aborn's "Turn Speed." And those are just half of the wonderful stories in this collection.

One of the recurrent themes of noir has always been the search for home. Not home in the physical sense—though that does happen—but in the irrational, emotional sense. The heroes and heroines of noir are usually chasing something they couldn't hold even if they caught up to it. Some part of them understands the futility of this chase even as another part clings to the need for it. This is probably why, if only to alleviate the pain of waiting, they chase something else in the meantime—a lover, a bank job, the murder of an inconvenient spouse. Yet the home being searched for in these pages might be Boston, and the journey to find it—however fruitless that goal may turn out to be—is as rich and varied, as hilarious and sad, and ultimately as engaging as the city itself.

Dennis Lehane
Boston, MA
July 2009

PART I

FEAR & LOATHING

EXIT INTERVIEW

BY LYNNE HEITMAN

Financial District

I t had been one of those weird sticky cool summer days
in downtown Boston, the kind that are as hot and humid as they're supposed to be until the breeze blows in
off the water and all of a sudden it's freezing cold and the
air stinks of salt and fish and brine. Sloan hates days that
start out one way and then turn into something else. They
make it harder to dress for work. She had spent most of
last night trying to decide what to wear to the office today.
Around 3 a.m., she'd settled on the pink summer-weight
St. John knit instead of the blue Tahari because Mother
loves the St. John. Says it makes her look svelte. Too bad
Mother won't get to see that she's wearing it for her big day.
She tugs the skirt up around her waist, but it sags back and
settles on her hip bones. This suit has never really fit, and
the dark blue Tahari would have hidden the bloodstains
better.

The steady churning of the helicopters grows louder.
Sloan flattens against the wall and peeks out into the night
from behind one of Trevor's fancy Japanese shades. With the
interior lights blazing, all she can see is her own reflection
staring back. More than once she has wanted to rip those silly
shades from Trevor's windows because who has an office on
the thirty-seventh floor and covers up the view? Tonight, as
flimsy as they are, she is glad to have them.

Her stomach cramps hard and doubles her over. She slides to the floor, which is where Trevor lies faceup, staring at the ceiling with the same look of surprise he died with. Sloan had never seen anyone die, not before today, but she's been to plenty of funerals. She always assumed that the way you look in the casket is the way you looked when your life ended. But she's had time to ponder this and it's now making sense to her. Once you're dead, you're dead. The light goes out and there is no time, no spark, no thought or impulse left to change the expression of absolute terror or disbelief or regret—whatever you were feeling the moment the bullet entered your brain and blew half of it out the gigantic hole in the back of your skull.

Her cell phone erupts in what had been until today her favorite Bach sonata. She taps the earpiece. "You said I had twenty minutes."

"You do, you do. I'm not trying to rush you. I'm just sayin' it doesn't mean we can't do it in less. Or that we can't spend the twenty minutes talkin'."

"I need that time. I need to think. I need . . ." It burns where the earpiece's hook has irritated the layer of soft skin around the top of her ear. These things were never meant to be worn for five straight hours.

"Talk to me, Sloan. What's going on up there?"

She wishes she could see her hostage negotiator, but she doesn't know where he is. He can somehow see her, though. She's sure of it. Thinking about him watching over her makes her feel calmer, but he has the frustrating habit of asking the same questions over and over.

"I think you know, Officer Tarbox, that what's—"

"When did we switch back to *Officer Tarbox?*"

"What's going on in here, Jimmy, is the same thing that's

been going on for the past five hours, and you promised me another half hour ten minutes ago."

"I'll keep my word. You know I will. Have I let you down any? Have I lied to you even once? No. I'm just checking in to see how you are. I want to know that you're okay and that everything's still on track. If we're not talkin', I don't know what's goin' on."

"You just want to know how Beck is."

"How is Beck?"

She glances over at Cornelius Beckwith Nash III, graduate of Exeter, Yale School of Drama, and Harvard Business School; Olympic rowing team alternate and scratch golfer; lead manager on the biggest portfolio of the growth team at Crowninshield Investment Management Company. Yet as impressive as he is, she's not sure any of those experiences have prepared him for being lashed to a chair for five hours with a telephone cord and computer cables. He's also sitting in his own sewage, which can't be comfortable, but it was his own fault for coming into the office to investigate instead of running the other way. He'd soiled his pants almost the second he'd walked in. Between that and Trevor's brains on the wall, the room smells worse than any paddock she's ever been in. But you can put up with anything, Sloan has learned, if you have to. You just can't put up with it forever.

"Beck is fine."

"Good. That's good. Can I talk to him?"

"No."

"Why not?"

Because she doesn't want to hear any more about little Max and littler Ian and if she takes off Beck's gag, all he'll do is cry about how his sons need him and how they'll miss him, and she already knows everything she needs to know about little Max and littler Ian. They go to Fessenden, spend summers on Nantucket eating watermelon, and will one day grow up to be strapping blond boys of privilege from the finest business schools who, given the chance, will pass her by. Just as their father had. But she doesn't like it when Officer Jimmy is not happy with her, so she gets up from the floor keeping her knees closed and turned gracefully to the side, heads over to Beck, takes off the earpiece, and holds it in front of him.

"Make some kind of noise."

The corners of Beck's mouth are split and caked with blood and dried spit where his $200 Zegna tie-gag is pinching. She knows he can moan—he's been doing it on and off for hours—but right now he seems comatose, frozen with his eyes open.

She shakes the earpiece. "Do it." But he doesn't and now she has to figure out how to make him. She hates the idea of touching him. The gun would be good for that. It's too heavy to carry around, so she keeps putting it down. Right now it's on Trevor's desk. But Beck is reading her mind. Before she even moves, he rolls out a few dry croaks and she wonders if the back of his throat is somehow pasted to the front.

"See?" She fits the earpiece back on her ear. "He's fine."

"All right," says Jimmy the officer. "That's good. Now we need to start talkin' about how to resolve this thing. We're at this five . . . going on six hours here, and you still haven't told me what you want."

"I was supposed to have half an hour to think about it and you only gave me ten minutes."

"You know we can't let this thing drag on forever." Only he says *forevah*. For all the things she likes about Jimmy Tarbox, the one thing that grates is his accent. "Let's talk about how to get you and Beck out of there without anyone else getting hurt. Let's figure this out together."

Sloan's stomach has settled, which means she can fall back into pacing the comfortable loop that runs between the conference table and the bookshelves, past the leather couch, the grandfather clock, and Beck, behind Trevor's desk, along his wall of photos, and back to the corner where the two walls of windows meet. Trevor is still wearing his raincoat and holding the handle of his soft leather briefcase in his right hand. Falling backwards, his left arm had hooked over one of his conference table chairs and pulled it down on top of him. His right leg is bent underneath him. He looks like a chalk outline. She steps over his head to get back on course.

"I can't come out. No one will understand what happened here."

"I understand. I know you didn't mean for all this to happen. You didn't get up this mornin' sayin', 'Today I'm going in to plug my boss.'"

"No." God no. This was supposed to have been the best day of her life. After picking the St. John suit, she had fallen into bed and actually slept for two hours. Waking refreshed, she had decided to forego the planned cab ride and walk to work instead. She usually walked for the exercise, but today she had noticed things. People in soft pants and flip-flops out on the Comm. Ave. Mall with their dogs, yawning and standing by with their baggies until there was a pile to clean up. The flowers in the Public Garden. Even the accordion-playing busker on the Common sounded good to her. She'd seen him there often, sitting on the same low brick wall under a tree, squeezing out sad French ballads, collecting tips from the well-dressed army of posers and wannabes making its weary way to the Financial

District for another day in the MUTUAL FUND CAPITAL OF THE *WORLD*! She had never given him a penny. She didn't believe in rewarding mediocrity. Also, he smelled.

But today she had admired his work ethic. Today she had slipped a twenty into his collection cup because everything was good and everyone was kind and even living in Boston wasn't so bad because today, after six long years in this second-rate backwater town, she would be named Managing Director. She would cross the magic line, get her ticket punched, and one day soon, get back home to New York where they would surely have to take her seriously now. Best of all, she would never again have to explain to Mother why Bo, James, and Danny had made MD before her. Sure they were two, four, and seven-and-a-half years younger, but they were also young, strapping boys from the finest business schools and the investment industry had no place for smart females—or any females—who didn't answer phones, fetch coffee, or give blowjobs to important clients.

"Sloan?"

"What?"

"Am I talkin' to myself here?" Officer Jimmy is making his point, but with a light touch, and she wishes she had learned how to be that way.

"You were saying it makes a difference if I hadn't planned on shooting Trevor today."

"Exactly. That it wasn't premeditated. We can work with that, and we can do some things here so the situation doesn't get worse than it is."

Uh-oh. Here it comes. She knows what he's about to say because he's said it a hundred times already.

"The biggest thing is you got to let Beck come out."

She breathes in deeply, pulling in the fetid and humid air

that has filled the office ever since they turned off the air conditioners. As they always seem to, her grinding molars find the scar tissue inside her left cheek and the taste in her mouth changes. She's bleeding.

"Why is everyone so concerned about Beck? Beck is fine. Beck is more than fine. *He* got promoted today. Or was it yesterday? He gets to be an MD, and do you know how long it took him? A year. I've been here six years and I've been up for MD the past four. Do you know who the biggest alpha generator around here is?"

"You?"

"For the past two years."

"What's an alpha?"

"Alpha generation . . . it's just a way of showing who earns the most for the firm, who the best stock picker is, and it's *me*. Do you know what they told me last year? 'We can't promote you because you're too volatile. Everyone's afraid of you.' And the year before that? 'We can't promote you because you're too quiet. No one ever knows what you're thinking.'"

"Take it easy. I'm not trying to upset you. I'm trying to get you to think through this thing logically with me. People will be coming to work in a few hours. You and me, we have to be done and out of here by then."

She takes a turn too fast and nearly bangs into the corner of Trevor's desk. She uncrosses her arms and takes her fists from her armpits. "Do you have any idea what it's like to be strung along year after year, to get your hopes up and then get told . . . to have to sit and be told all the things that are wrong with you?"

"No, I don't know what it's like to be in your position— your work position or the one you're in now. But I do know what it's like to get passed over. I got passed over for this job six times."

He's saying all the right words. He's saying he understands because that's his job. But she hears it in his tone. *You stupid bitch*, he's thinking. *You had everything—the money, the Back Bay condo, the friggin' horse farm in Millbrook. The shopping trips to London. And you do this? This is what you do? You stupid, spoiled rich little bitch.*

She grabs the earpiece, holds it directly in front of her mouth. "I made two and a half million dollars last year. What did *you* make?" Hits the button to end the call, and just like that Jimmy Tarbox is out of her head.

But her head throbs. From the heat, maybe. Or dehydration. She pushes back against it with the heels of her hands against her eyes. She holds her jacket open and fans it, trying to air out. All night she's resisted taking it off—she never takes her jacket off in public—but it has to come off. It's too hard to breathe. What to do about Beck? She goes over and grabs the high back of his chair. It annoys her that he doesn't flinch anymore when she approaches. She turns him to face the wall. He can stare at Trevor's collection of golf photos.

Instead of gliding off, the jacket's silk lining sticks to the damp insides of her elbows and she has to wrestle with it. Mother would be mortified. She settles it onto the hanger on the back of the door and stands with her arms wrapped around her. *Spider-arms* they used to call her, all the girls back at Monsignor Xavier Prep. She looks at Trevor's face. What had high school been like for him back in Manchester or Sheffield or wherever he was from? Probably no one ever called him names, but she didn't know. She didn't know much of anything about Trevor.

Bony Sloany. That was another one. She had hated high

school with every fiber in her bony body. Except for the stables. The horses and riding had saved her. These days, all that saves her is Rowan. She closes her eyes and tries to think of him. He can usually calm her down, but right now her head is too jammed.

When she opens her eyes, there is Beck. She should kill him. Put the gun to the back of his head, pull the trigger, and put him down, all without ever having to look upon his classically handsome face again. She's already killed Trevor. Why not just do it now and let this end?

Because she hadn't really thought it through with Trevor.

She'd caught him trying to sneak out of the building without talking to her. Not even sneaking. Just walking out as if she hadn't been sitting in her office all day waiting for his call. As if she hadn't skipped her daily caramel latte to cut down on trips to the bathroom. As if she hadn't spent the long hours of the afternoon rocking back and forth at her desk, staring at the blinking cursor on her Bloomberg screen, and pleading with God not to let it happen again because she could feel it happening again. Falling and falling, waiting to hit the concrete, picking up speed with every second that ticked by with no call from Trevor. So she had prayed, asking God not to let her have anything else taken away.

And then she'd heard the vacuum cleaner, and the vacuum cleaner only ran on her floor after 7 o'clock in the evening. She'd come out of her office to find the entire floor abandoned except for the summer intern—Hailey? Hallie?— huddled over the printer. She'd moved toward Trevor's office, slowing down as she went, not knowing if she was more afraid to find him there or gone. He was there, all right. Impossible to miss. Blustery blowhard Trevor holding forth. The voice on the other side of the conversation hadn't been as loud, but she had recognized it. Trevor and Beck talking, voices brimming with excitement and manly good cheer. The tone had been clear, but the words were covered by the sound of the approaching vacuum. She'd thought they might be talking golf.

Her phone is singing again. She reaches for the earpiece and finds nothing but ear. Can't remember taking the thing off. She follows the Bach and finds her cell on the conference table.

"Hello?"

"How you doing, kid?"

"Fine."

"How's Beck?"

"Same."

"I have to ask you to stop hanging up on me. The bosses are getting sick of this thing. You've got bosses. You know what I'm sayin', right?"

He's skipping over the fact that her boss is a corpse in a $6,000 Brioni suit and a TAG Heuer watch and that she's the one who made him that way. He's acting as if she could surrender to him and then go home tonight, eat a banana for dinner, maybe walk over to Emack & Bolio's for a scoop of fat-free vanilla yogurt in a cup. Make it last for an hour while she sits and watches the cool kids on Newbury Street smoking and laughing and texting. Then she could come in to work tomorrow, maybe wearing the dark blue Tahari, and show up at the morning meeting as if nothing had happened. Of course, Beck would be the new MD on the growth team, or maybe they would just slot him into Trevor's job as CIO and promote some other strapping young boy from a fine business school to MD. Pick any of them—Justin, Peter, Shamir. She'd still be a senior portfolio manager. She would always be a senior portfolio manager, which was why she'd had no choice but to take the .22 out of her bag and shoot Trevor through the head.

"I have to ask you this to make sure," Jimmy says. "Don't get upset, but your father keeps calling from New York. Are you sure you don't want to talk to him?"

She knows why Daddy is calling and she knows why Mother isn't. Mother is lying perfectly still in some dark room with a damp cloth on her forehead and a few dozen milligrams of Percocet coursing through her veins. Daddy would be more worried than upset. Worried about his cash flow. "Doesn't matter what they call you," he always tells her, usually in front of her MD brothers, "as long as the bonuses keep rolling in." Bo, James, and Danny were too smart or too selfish or both to keep investing in his hedge fund, which really meant tithing over some growing percentage of her annual bonus and calling it an investment so that Mother wouldn't be humiliated by another of Daddy's busted ventures. Eventually, Daddy had stopped asking her brothers for money. "They're married," he'd told her. "They have families of their own to feed."

Sloan's legs feel like dead weights, so heavy. She walks to the couch and crashes down. "I don't want to talk to him, and if you make me, I swear I will hang up and you will never hear from me again."

"I can't make you do anything, remember? You're in charge. We're doing things your way."

"Then stop asking. Tell him to stop calling."

"Consider it done. Is there anyone you want to talk to? Who's this Rowan?"

She smiles, envisioning Officer Jimmy thumbing quickly through a stack of background information on her that someone has dumped in his lap. "My horse."

"Your horse?" There is shuffling and mumbling. "Okay, I

see it here now. Holy smokes, he's a beauty. Is he at your horse farm?" More shuffling. "Where is this Millbrook anyway?"

"New York."

"New York is a big state and I'm sitting here without my Google."

That's a lie. He's probably sitting there with every possible source of data at his disposal, but she doesn't mind playing along with Officer Jimmy. "It's in the eastern part of the state, close to the Connecticut border."

"How long's it take you to get out there?"

"Three and a half hours."

"You just go 90 west?"

"To Route 22."

"Yeah, I have no idea where that is."

"If you keep going on 22 you get to Poughkeepsie."

"If you say so. How often do you get out there?"

"Every weekend."

"Wow. You must really like the place."

There isn't a word strong enough to describe how she feels out there. Millbrook is her escape. She makes the drive every Friday after work, rain or shine, happy or sad. She stays through Sunday night and drives straight to work on Monday. There is space out there. There is grass and air that smells nice. In the winter there is clean snow that stretches on forever.

And Rowan.

She closes her eyes and conjures him. She smells his barn and feels him moving under her hands as she curries his withers. The grooms always put him on the crossties to clean him, but not Sloan. She scratches all his favorite places and smiles when he curls his neck around to give her a playful nudge every time she finds another with the hard bristles. Then she rides him and feels his calm and coiled anticipation as he gathers himself for a jump, then the explosion, the thrust high into the air and that feeling of flying, just Rowan and her, her face so close that his mane brushes her cheek.

She pushes at the tears with the back of her hand and gets to her feet. "I'm turning off the lights. It's too hot in here. I'm also putting up one of the blinds, just so you know."

"Just so *you* know, I don't control the snipers. I'm not the one in charge of the scene."

"I don't even have the gun. It's on Trevor's standing desk." She looks around for her earpiece so she can have both hands free, hopes the battery hasn't run down.

"What the hell is a standing desk?"

"All the CIOs have them. It's a power thing."

"What's a CIO?"

"Chief Investment Officer." She finds the earpiece on the floor near Beck's chair and switches the call over. "But Trevor didn't want one like everyone else, so he . . . actually, he had his assistant Nicole do all the research and she found this mahogany antique that was used by Charles Dickens. It cost the firm over $100,000 to have it restored and shipped from London."

"A hundred grand? Jeez, that would have covered both my kids' college tuition."

The light switch is by the door. This time as she passes Trevor, she reaches down and tips the chair off of him, setting it back on its feet. She flips the lights off and feels instantly better, cooler. She rolls up one of the fancy shades and then, what the hell, does them all. She opens all the windows of the corner office to the nighttime view. It is magnificent, even at 2 o'clock in the morning. She feels as if she's floating out over the harbor, just another of the lights moving across the water. They must be ships, those lights, and she wonders what life would be like living on a moving vessel. Logan has airport lights: red ones, green ones, bright beacons, flashing fast and slow. The runway lights look like jeweled bracelets laid out on a black velvet pillow.

The glass window feels cool, so she presses her cheek against it, the side without the earpiece. "Will the snipers shoot me?"

"Why would they shoot you while we're still talkin'? And so long as you're leaving Beck alone? How is Beck? Does he need any water?"

"Do you care what happens to me?"

"I've spent all night talkin' to you. What do you think?"

"I think you care about what happens to Beck."

"I do. And I care about what happens to you. That's no bullshit. I want you to walk out of there."

Trevor's body is hard to see in the dark, but she knows it's there. "Why would you care? Why would anyone care? I'm a murderer." She's been trying all night to feel the weight of that word and how to wear it. Mostly she feels how Mother will wear it.

"Listen, kid, I deal with all kinds in this job. I can tell the wackos and I can tell the ones that just got pushed too far. You get pushed around and pushed around until you can't do it anymore and then something happens. It's just a wrong-place-wrong-time-bad-chain-of-events kind of a deal, and if one thing had gone different yesterday, maybe none of this happens. Am I right?"

The sky is another sight to behold. The moon lights the clouds from behind, making them seem transparent and solid at the same time as they rush through space.

"What are the names of the islands, Jimmy?"

"What islands?"

"Isn't there something out there called the Harbor Islands?" She's seen them a thousand times from Trevor's office.

"Sure, but there's somethin' like forty"—*fawty*—"of 'em out there. You never went to any of them?"

"I never did. Tell me some of the names."

"Long Island, Sheep Island . . . There's a little one called Grape. I went swimming once with my brothers at Spectacle. It used to have great beaches, but then the city used it for dumping all the Big Dig dirt, so I don't know what it's like now. Deer Island is where they have the shit plant."

"Excuse me?"

"Sewage plant. One of the Brewsters has the oldest lighthouse ever. Georges Island has a Civil War fort. I went to both of those on school field trips when I was a kid. There's a Sarah's Island. I always remember it because that was my ma's name."

"Where are you from?"

"Haverhill."

"Where are you right now?"

"I can't tell you that."

She scans the building at State Street and Congress, the only one tall enough for him to be looking down at her. But it's a huge black mirrored tower that reveals nothing. "Can I see you?"

"I'll spend all the time in the world with you, but you gotta let Beck come out of there. And you need to come out too. What you have to keep in mind is that you're still young and you deserve to come out of there in one piece. You need to give yourself that chance."

Another requirement. Another trade-off. Another contingent offer. She slides down the window and sits with her back to the north, looking out over the water. "Was it supposed to rain today, Jimmy?"

"If it was supposed to, it never did."

"It just struck me as so odd that he was wearing a raincoat because I hadn't heard anything about rain today and the whole time we were having our meeting he never took it off."

"Trevor?"

"I was standing outside his office listening to him talking to Beck. And then Beck came out and I wanted to go in. I assumed it was my turn, that he was just running late with his meetings. I didn't want to look too eager, so I went to my office and packed my things and came back."

"Make it look all casual, huh? Like you were just leaving and stopped by."

"I was standing there trying to get up the courage to walk in, then he walked out and nearly ran me over. He wasn't happy to see me, I could tell, but he wouldn't show it. You know what he said? 'Brilliant!' As if it was a stroke of grand good luck that I was standing right there. 'Of course I'm still here, you bastard. You told me yesterday not to leave today without seeing you because you would have good news for me, which is why I spent the entire day locked in my office afraid to go to the bathroom, because I was waiting for you to call me, you pompous, self-centered ass.'"

"You said that to him?" Officer Jimmy's voice holds a hint of respect, and for a moment Sloan feels as if they really are buddies in a foxhole. But she hadn't actually said any of those things to Trevor.

"We came into the office and he stood behind his desk."

"His hundred-thousand-dollar standing desk?"

"I've never seen him use that. No, he stood behind his sitting desk, but he didn't sit and I could tell he didn't want me to sit, but I did anyway. Then he opened his desk drawer and without looking reached in and took out an envelope, and I tried as hard as I could to come up with a good reason why my bonus check was the only one left in the drawer, and why it was after 7 o'clock and the only reason he was talking to me at all was because I'd caught him trying to slip out, and why if it was good news he hadn't already given it to me."

"I hear you."

"When he pushed the envelope across the desk, he gave me one of his looks where he cocks up an eyebrow. 'I think you'll be very pleased with that.'" She tries to capture not just his accent, but his condescending tone. "I just sat there with this pain in my stomach and a horrible sensation running up and down my back and I thought . . . I really thought I was just going to die sitting right there waiting for him to tell me."

"You sound like you were in shock."

"But he just stood there, still in his raincoat, doing one of those things where you glance at your watch without wanting someone to see that you're doing it."

"Prick."

"Then he said, 'Aren't you going to open it?' and I said, 'I didn't get it, did I? I didn't get MD.' He looked at me and I could see what he was thinking right on his face. *You bitch. You ungrateful little cunt.* I know that's what he was thinking because I've heard him say that word before and he wasn't even trying to hide it, how much he hated me. How much he loathed me for not letting him go home or to the cigar bar or . . . wherever. That's when I knew."

"What did you know?"

"That I was never going to get MD."

Sloan pushes herself up from the floor, but falls back against the window. Her skirt comes all the way up her thighs as she tries to find her balance. No food for almost two days.

No water since early afternoon. The heat. It's all starting to catch up with her and she'll pass out soon. She finally makes it to her feet.

"No matter how good I was, no matter how much money I made for them, they were going to keep telling me I was *this close* and to hang in there and that next year would be my year. And then next year would come around and they'd promote someone like Beck because they like Beck and they can talk about golf with him."

One by one, she pulls the shades down.

"What are you doing up there, Sloan. What's going on now?"

Maybe she's memorized this room, because how else can she walk across the office through the dark without bumping into things? She finds the gun on the standing desk.

"Talk to me, kid. I need to hear you."

"Trevor told me he had this wired. He told me there was no way I wasn't getting it, that this was my year. When I reminded him of this, he said, 'Who can fathom what goes on behind those closed doors? Certainly I can't. One answer goes in and a different answer comes out. It's damn confounding, *damn* confounding, but you can't take it personally.'"

"He's still a prick, but what are you doing?"

"That's when I started to think about it. I wanted to kill him. I wanted to grab him by his tie and squeeze until his head popped off, which wasn't a real option. But I did have the gun."

"Do you have the gun now?"

"You know how you just said that if one thing had gone differently yesterday, maybe none of this would have happened?"

"Yes."

"It was Sunday. The thing that happened. I had to use the

LYNNE HEITMAN // 35

gun on Sunday in Millbrook. It was still in my travel bag. I forgot to take it out, so there it was."

Officer Jimmy says nothing for a few seconds. "You didn't hurt anybody out in Millbrook, did you?"

The tears come again. She tries to hold them back—she's never cried in front of anyone—but it's no use, and then she's wailing into Officer Jimmy's ear. "The only one who got hurt out there was me."

She's standing behind Beck now, looking over his shoulder at Trevor's framed photos on the wall. There's a light from somewhere, because she can see it clearly, the one he was most proud of: Trevor with Nick Price. The first time she'd ever heard of Nick Price was the first time she'd been in Trevor's office, the day of her first interview. The pro golfer, he'd explained, patiently filling in the unfortunate gaps in her knowledge. "Nicest guy you'd ever want to meet" is what he'd said. Later she'd learned that it was what he said to everyone who came into his office. Price had written in bold black strokes across his own red shirt, *To Trevor, Keep your head down, my friend. All the best, Nick.*

Sloan couldn't hear anything, too much noise outside, but she could see Beck struggling. He couldn't see her, but he must have sensed her standing behind him with the gun. "He won the British Open," Sloan says, repeating to Jimmy what Trevor had said to her at just the wrong moment, in just the wrong tone. If he had just taken off his raincoat . . .

"Who did?"

"I was sitting in my chair completely devastated. I couldn't stand to look at Trevor, so I looked past him and I must have been staring at Nick Price and it occurred to me that Beck had gotten MD." Her hands shook so much she had a hard time releasing the safety. "I didn't get MD. Beck did. That's what they were talking about. That's what they were laughing about."

"I'm hearing you, Sloan, but you have to slow things down. Do me a favor and take a breath. Please."

"I've decided what I want, Jimmy."

"Tell me."

"I want you to mix my ashes with Rowan's."

Officer Jimmy is breathing harder now. She pictures him standing, maybe doing some pacing of his own. "Don't start talkin' like that. No one's going to be ashes at the end of this because then I'm going to look bad and neither one of us wants that." He tries for one of his light chuckles but it's not like before. "Besides, you don't want anything happening to that beautiful horse of yours."

"He's dead."

For the first time in their conversation, Officer Jimmy has nothing to say. Then, finally, "What happened?"

"He spooked. He ran into a car and I had—" She tries for a breath, but it catches in her chest. "I called the vet but it took too long and he was so broken and suffering too much and I couldn't watch him like that so I had to—" Her head pounds with the effort to get each word out, but she's determined. No more requirements. No more contingencies. "I put him down. He was never going to be all right again. I had to put him down." This time when she takes a breath the air goes deep, and she feels calm. Rowan could always calm her down. "His ashes are in the box on the table in my condo."

"Okay, I know what you're thinking. You're thinking there's nothing left for you, right? You're thinking there's no way outta this, but it's not true . . ."

Jimmy's voice fades away. When did this gun get so heavy? She can barely lift it. "Do one other thing, Officer Jimmy."

She presses the barrel against her forehead, puts both thumbs on the trigger. "Please tell Trevor's family that I'm sorry." She closes her eyes and thinks about Rowan.

"*Go! Go! Go! Go!*"

The door explodes behind her. Her hands stop shaking. She holds the gun steady and pulls the trigger.

ANIMAL RESCUE

BY DENNIS LEHANE

Dorchester

Bob found the dog in the trash.

It was just after Thanksgiving, the neighborhood gone quiet, hungover. After bartending at Cousin Marv's, Bob sometimes walked the streets. He was big and lumpy and hair had been growing in unlikely places all over his body since his teens. In his twenties, he'd fought against the hair, carrying small clippers in his coat pocket and shaving twice a day. He'd also fought the weight, but during all those years of fighting, no girl who wasn't being paid for it ever showed any interest in him. After a time, he gave up the fight. He lived alone in the house he grew up in, and when it seemed likely to swallow him with its smells and memories and dark couches, the attempts he'd made to escape it—through church socials, lodge picnics, and one horrific mixer thrown by a dating service—had only opened the wound further, left him patching it back up for weeks, cursing himself for hoping.

So he took these walks of his and, if he was lucky, sometimes he forgot people lived any other way. That night, he paused on the sidewalk, feeling the ink sky above him and the cold in his fingers, and he closed his eyes against the evening.

He was used to it. He was used to it. It was okay.

You could make a friend of it, as long as you didn't fight it.

With his eyes closed, he heard it—a worn-out keening

accompanied by distant scratching and a sharper, metallic rattling. He opened his eyes. Fifteen feet down the sidewalk, a large metal barrel with a heavy lid shook slightly under the yellow glare of the streetlight, its bottom scraping the sidewalk. He stood over it and heard that keening again, the sound of a creature that was one breath away from deciding it was too hard to take the next, and he pulled off the lid.

He had to remove some things to get to it—a toaster and five thick Yellow Pages, the oldest dating back to 2000. The dog—either a very small one or else a puppy—was down at the bottom, and it scrunched its head into its midsection when the light hit it. It exhaled a soft chug of a whimper and tightened its body even more, its eyes closed to slits. A scrawny thing. Bob could see its ribs. He could see a big crust of dried blood by its ear. No collar. It was brown with a white snout and paws that seemed far too big for its body.

It let out a sharper whimper when Bob reached down, sank his fingers into the nape of its neck, and lifted it out of its own excrement. Bob didn't know dogs too well, but there was no mistaking this one for anything but a boxer. And definitely a puppy, the wide brown eyes opening and looking into his as he held it up before him.

Somewhere, he was sure, two people made love. A man and a woman. Entwined. Behind one of those shades, oranged with light, that looked down on the street. Bob could feel them in there, naked and blessed. And he stood out here in the cold with a near-dead dog staring back at him. The icy sidewalk glinted like new marble, and the wind was dark and gray as slush.

"What do you got there?"

Bob turned, looked up and down the sidewalk.

"I'm up here. And you're in my trash."

She stood on the front porch of the three-decker nearest him. She'd turned the porch light on and stood there shivering, her feet bare. She reached into the pocket of her hoodie and came back with a pack of cigarettes. She watched him as she got one going.

"I found a dog." Bob held it up.

"A *what?*"

"A dog. A puppy. A boxer, I think."

She coughed out some smoke. "Who puts a dog in a barrel?"

"Right?" he said. "It's bleeding." He took a step toward her stairs and she backed up.

"Who do you know that I would know?" A city girl, not about to just drop her guard around a stranger.

"I don't know," Bob said. "How about Francie Hedges?"

She shook her head. "You know the Sullivans?"

That wouldn't narrow it down. Not around here. You shook a tree, a Sullivan fell out. Followed by a six-pack most times. "I know a bunch."

This was going nowhere, the puppy looking at him, shaking worse than the girl.

"Hey," she said, "you live in this parish?"

"Next one over. St. Theresa's."

"Go to church?"

"Most Sundays."

"So you know Father Pete?"

"Pete Regan," he said, "sure."

She produced a cell phone. "What's your name?"

"Bob," he said. "Bob Saginowski."

Bob waited as she stepped back from the light, phone to one ear, finger pressed into the other. He stared at the puppy. The puppy stared back, like, How did I get *here?* Bob touched its nose with his index finger. The puppy blinked its huge eyes. For a moment, Bob couldn't recall his sins.

"Nadia," the girl said and stepped back into the light. "Bring him up here, Bob. Pete says hi."

They washed it in Nadia's sink, dried it off, and brought it to her kitchen table.

Nadia was small. A bumpy red rope of a scar ran across the base of her throat like the smile of a drunk circus clown. She had a tiny moon of a face, savaged by pockmarks, and small, heart-pendant eyes. Shoulders that didn't cut so much as dissolve at the arms. Elbows like flattened beer cans. A yellow bob of hair curled on either side of her face. "It's not a boxer." Her eyes glanced off Bob's face before dropping the puppy back onto her kitchen table. "It's an American Staffordshire terrier."

Bob knew he was supposed to understand something in her tone, but he didn't know what that thing was so he remained silent.

She glanced back up at him after the quiet lasted too long. "A pit bull."

"That's a pit bull?"

She nodded and swabbed the puppy's head wound again. Someone had pummeled it, she told Bob. Probably knocked it unconscious, assumed it was dead, and dumped it.

"Why?" Bob said.

She looked at him, her round eyes getting rounder, wider. "Just because." She shrugged, went back to examining the dog. "I worked at Animal Rescue once. You know the place on Shawmut? As a vet tech. Before I decided it wasn't my thing. They're so hard, this breed . . ."

"What?"

"To adopt out," she said. "It's very hard to find them a home."

"I don't know about dogs. I never had a dog. I live alone. I was just walking by the barrel." Bob found himself beset by a desperate need to explain himself, explain his life. "I'm just not . . ." He could hear the wind outside, black and rattling. Rain or bits of hail spit against the windows.

Nadia lifted the puppy's back left paw—the other three paws were brown, but this one was white with peach spots. Then she dropped the paw as if it were contagious. She went back to the head wound, took a closer look at the right ear, a piece missing from the tip that Bob hadn't noticed until now.

"Well," she said, "he'll live. You're gonna need a crate and food and all sorts of stuff."

"No," Bob said. "You don't understand."

She cocked her head, gave him a look that said she understood perfectly.

"I can't. I just found him. I was gonna give him back."

"To whoever beat him, left him for dead?"

"No, no, like, the authorities."

"That would be Animal Rescue," she said. "After they give the owner seven days to reclaim him, they'll—"

"The guy who beat him? He gets a second chance?"

She gave him a half-frown and a nod. "*If* he doesn't take it," she lifted the puppy's ear, peered in, "chances are this little fella'll be put up for adoption. But it's hard. To find them a home. Pit bulls. More often than not?" She looked at Bob. "More often than not, they're put down."

Bob felt a wave of sadness roll out from her that immediately shamed him. He didn't know how, but he'd caused pain. He'd put some out into the world. He'd let this girl down. "I . . ." he started. "It's just . . ."

She glanced up at him. "I'm sorry?"

Bob looked at the puppy. Its eyes were droopy from a long day in the barrel and whoever gave it that wound. It had stopped shivering, though.

"You can take it," Bob said. "You used to work there, like you said. You—"

She shook her head. "My father lives with me. He gets home Sunday night from Foxwoods. He finds a dog in his house? An animal he's allergic to?" She jerked her thumb. "Puppy goes back in the barrel."

"Can you give me till Sunday morning?" Bob wasn't sure how it was the words left his mouth, since he couldn't remember formulating them or even thinking them.

The girl eyed him carefully. "You're not just saying it? Cause, I shit you not, he ain't picked up by Sunday noon, he's back out that door."

"Sunday, then." Bob said the words with a conviction he actually felt. "Sunday, definitely."

"Yeah?" She smiled, and it was a spectacular smile, and Bob saw that the face behind the pockmarks was as spectacular as the smile. Wanting only to be seen. She touched the puppy's nose with her index finger.

"Yeah." Bob felt crazed. He felt light as a communion wafer. "Yeah."

At Cousin Marv's, where he tended bar 12 to 10, Wednesday through Sunday, he told Marv all about it. Most people called Marv *Cousin* Marv out of habit, something that went back to grade school though no one could remember how, but Marv actually was Bob's cousin. On his mother's side.

Cousin Marv had run a crew in the late '80s and early '90s. It had been primarily comprised of guys with interests in the loaning and subsequent debt-repayal side of things, though Marv never turned his nose down at any paying proposition because he believed, to the core of his soul, that those who failed to diversify were always the first to collapse when the wind turned. Like the dinosaurs, he'd say to Bob, when the cavemen came along and invented arrows. Picture the cavemen, he'd say, firing away, and the tyrannosauruses all gucked up in the oil puddles. A tragedy so easily averted.

Marv's crew hadn't been the toughest crew or the smartest or the most successful operating in the neighborhood—not even close—but for a while they got by. Other crews kept nipping at their heels, though, and except for one glaring exception, they'd never been ones to favor violence. Pretty soon, they had to make the decision to yield to crews a lot meaner than they were or duke it out. They took Door Number One.

Marv's income derived from running his bar as a drop. In the new world order—a loose collective of Chechen, Italian, and Irish hard guys—no one wanted to get caught with enough merch or enough money for a case to go Federal. So they kept it out of their offices and out of their homes and they kept it on the move. About every two-three weeks, drops were made at Cousin Marv's, among other establishments. You sat on the drop for a night, two at the most, before some beer-truck driver showed up with the weekend's password and hauled everything back out on a dolly like it was a stack of empty kegs, took it away in a refrigerated semi. The rest of Marv's income derived from being a fence, one of the best in the city, but being a fence in their world (or a drop bar operator for that matter) was like being a mailroom clerk in the straight world—if you were still doing it after thirty, it was all you'd ever do. For Bob, it was a relief—he liked being a bartender and he'd hated that one time they'd had to come heavy. Marv, though, Marv still waited for the golden train to arrive on the golden tracks, take him away from all this. Most times, he pretended to be happy. But Bob knew that the things that haunted Marv were the same things that haunted Bob—the shitty things you did to get ahead. Those things laughed at you if your ambitions failed to amount to much; a successful man could hide his past; an unsuccessful man sat in his.

That morning, Marv was looking a hair on the mournful side, lighting one Camel while the previous one still smoldered, so Bob tried to cheer him up by telling him about his adventure with the dog. Marv didn't seem too interested, and Bob found himself saying "You had to be there" so much, he eventually shut up about it.

Marv said, "Rumor is we're getting the Super Bowl drop."

"No shit?"

If true (an enormous *if*), this was huge. They worked on commission—one half of one percent of the drop. A Super Bowl drop? It would be like one half of one percent of Exxon.

Natalie's scar flashed in Bob's brain, the redness of it, the thick, ropey texture. "They send extra guys to protect it, you think?"

Marv rolled his eyes. "Why, cause people are just lining up to steal from coked-up Chechnyans."

"Chechens," Bob said.

"But they're from Chechnya."

Bob shrugged. "I think it's like how you don't call people from Ireland *Irelandians*."

Marv scowled. "Whatever. It means all this hard work we've been doing? It's paid off. Like how Toyota did it, making friends and influencing people."

Bob kept quiet. If they ended up being the drop for the Super Bowl, it was because someone figured out no Feds deemed them important enough to be watched. But in Marv's fantasies, the crew (long since dispersed to straight jobs, jail, or, worse, Connecticut) could regain its glory days, even though those days had lasted about as long as a Swatch. It never occurred to Marv that one day they'd come take everything he had—the fence, the money and merch he kept in the safe in back, hell, the bar probably—just because they were sick of him hanging around, looking at them with needy expectation. It had gotten so every time he talked about the "people he knew," the dreams he had, Bob had to resist the urge to reach for the 9mm they kept beneath the bar and blow his own brains out. Not really—but close sometimes. Man, Marv could wear you out.

A guy stuck his head in the bar, late twenties but with white hair, a white goatee, a silver stud in his ear. He dressed like most kids these days—like shit: pre-ripped jeans, slovenly T-shirt under a faded hoodie under a wrinkled wool topcoat. He didn't cross the threshold, just craned his head in, the cold day pouring in off the sidewalk behind him.

"Help you?" Bob asked.

The guy shook his head, kept staring at the gloomy bar like it was a crystal ball.

"Mind shutting the door?" Marv didn't look up. "Cold out there."

"You serve Zima?" The guy's eyes flew around the bar, up and down, left to right.

Marv looked up now. "Who the fuck would we serve it to—Moesha?"

The guy raised an apologetic hand. "My bad." He left, and the warmth returned with the closing of the door.

Marv said, "You know that kid?"

Bob shook his head. "Mighta seen him around but I can't place him."

"He's a fucking nutbag. Lives in the next parish, probably why you don't know him. You're old school that way, Bob—somebody didn't go to parochial school with you, it's like they don't exist."

Bob couldn't argue. When he'd been a kid, your parish was your country. Everything you needed and needed to know was contained within it. Now that the archdiocese had shuttered half the parishes to pay for the crimes of the kid-diddler priests, Bob couldn't escape the fact that those days of parish dominion, long dwindling, were gone. He was a certain type of guy, of a certain half-generation, an almost generation, and while there were still plenty of them left, they were older, grayer, they had smokers' coughs, they went in for checkups and never checked back out.

"That kid?" Marv gave Bob a bump of his eyebrows. "They say he killed Richie Whelan back in the day."

"*They* say?"

"They do."

"Well, then . . ."

They sat in silence for a bit. Snow-dust blew past the window in the high-pitched breeze. The street signs and window panes rattled, and Bob thought how winter lost any meaning the day you last rode a sled. Any meaning but gray. He looked into the unlit sections of the barroom. The shadows became hospital beds, stooped old widowers shopping for sympathy cards, empty wheelchairs. The wind howled a little sharper.

"This puppy, right?" Bob said. "He's got paws the size of his head. Three are brown but one's white with these little peach-colored spots over the white. And—"

"This thing cook?" Marv said. "Clean the house? I mean, it's a fucking dog."

"Yeah, but it was—" Bob dropped his hands. He didn't know how to explain. "You know that feeling you get some-times on a really great day? Like, like, the Pats dominate and you took the 'over,' or they cook your steak just right up the Blarney, or, or you just feel *good*? Like . . ." Bob found himself waving his hands again ". . . good?"

Marv gave him a nod and a tight smile. Went back to his racing sheet.

On Sunday morning, Nadia brought the puppy to his car as he idled in front of her house. She handed it through the window and gave them both a little wave.

He looked at the puppy sitting on his seat and fear washed over him. What does it eat? When does it eat? Housebreak-ing. How do you do that? How long does it take? He'd had days to consider these questions—why were they only occur-ring to him now?

He hit the brakes and reversed the car a few feet. Nadia, one foot on her bottom step, turned back. He rolled down the passenger window, craned his body across the seat until he was peering up at her.

"I don't know what to do," he said. "I don't know any-thing."

At a supermarket for pets, Nadia picked out several chew toys, told Bob he'd need them if he wanted to keep his couch. Shoes, she told him, keep your shoes hidden from now on, up on a high shelf. They bought vitamins—for a dog!—and a bag of puppy food she recommended, telling him the most important thing was to stick with that brand from now on. Change a dog's diet, she warned, you'll get piles of diarrhea on your floor.

They got a crate to put him in when Bob was at work. They got a water bottle for the crate and a book on dog training written by monks who were on the cover looking hardy and not real monkish, big smiles. As the cashier rang it all up, Bob felt a quake rumble through his body, a momentary disruption as he reached for his wallet. His throat flushed with heat. His head felt fizzy. And only as the quake went away and his throat cooled and his head cleared and he handed over his credit card to the cashier did he realize, in the sudden disappearance of the feeling, what the feeling had been: for a moment—maybe even a succession of moments, and none sharp enough to point to as the cause—he'd been happy.

"So, thank you," she said when he pulled up in front of her house.

"What? No. Thank *you*. Please. Really. It . . . Thank you."

She said, "This little guy, he's a good guy. He's going to make you proud, Bob."

He looked down at the puppy, sleeping on her lap now, snoring slightly. "Do they do that? Sleep all the time?"

"Pretty much. Then they run around like loonies for about twenty minutes. Then they sleep some more. And poop. Bob, man, you got to remember that—they poop and pee like crazy. Don't get mad. They don't know any better. Read the monk book. It takes time, but they figure out soon enough not to do it in the house."

"What's soon enough?"

"Two months?" She cocked her head. "Maybe three. Be patient, Bob."

"Be patient," he repeated.

"And you too," she said to the puppy as she lifted it off her lap. He came awake, sniffing, snorting. He didn't want her to go. "You *both* take care." She let herself out and gave Bob a wave as she walked up her steps, then went inside.

The puppy was on its haunches, staring up at the window like Nadia might reappear there. It looked back over his shoulder at Bob. Bob could feel its abandonment. He could feel his own. He was certain they'd make a mess of it, him and this throwaway dog. He was sure the world was too strong.

"What's your name?" he asked the puppy. "What are we going to call you?"

The puppy turned his head away, like, Bring the girl back.

First thing it did was take a shit in the dining room.

Bob didn't even realize what it was doing at first. It started sniffing, nose scraping the rug, and then it looked up at Bob with an air of embarrassment. And Bob said, "What?" and the dog dumped all over the corner of the rug.

Bob scrambled forward, as if he could stop it, push it back in, and the puppy bolted, left droplets on the hardwood as it scurried into the kitchen.

Bob said, "No, no. It's okay." Although it wasn't. Most everything in the house had been his mother's, largely unchanged since she'd purchased it in the '50s. That was shit. Excrement. In his mother's house. On her rug, her floor.

In the seconds it took him to reach the kitchen, the puppy'd left a piss puddle on the linoleum. Bob almost slipped in it. The puppy was sitting against the fridge, looking at him, tensing for a blow, trying not to shake.

And it stopped Bob. It stopped him even as he knew the longer he left the shit on the rug, the harder it would be to get out.

Bob got down on all fours. He felt the sudden return of what he'd felt when he first picked it out of the trash, something he'd assumed had left with Nadia. Connection. He suspected they might have been brought together by something other than chance.

He said, "Hey." Barely above a whisper. "Hey, it's all right." So, so slowly, he extended his hand, and the puppy pressed itself harder against the fridge. But Bob kept the hand coming, and gently lay his palm on the side of the animal's face. He made soothing sounds. He smiled at it. "It's okay," he repeated, over and over.

He named it Cassius because he'd mistaken it for a boxer and he liked the sound of the word. It made him think of Roman legions, proud jaws, honor.

Nadia called him Cash. She came around after work sometimes and she and Bob took it on walks. He knew something was a little off about Nadia—the dog being found so close to her house and her lack of surprise or interest in that fact was not lost on Bob—but was there anyone, anywhere on this planet, who wasn't a little off? More than a little most times. Nadia came by to help with the dog and Bob, who hadn't known much friendship in his life, took what he could get.

They taught Cassius to sit and lie down and paw and roll over. Bob read the entire monk book and followed its instructions. The puppy had his rabies shot and was cleared of any cartilage damage to his ear. Just a bruise, the vet said, just a deep bruise. He grew fast.

Weeks passed without Cassius having an accident, but Bob still couldn't be sure whether that was luck or not, and then on Super Bowl Sunday, Cassius used one paw on the back door. Bob let him out and then tore through the house to call Nadia. He was so proud he felt like yodeling, and he almost mistook the doorbell for something else. A kettle, he thought, still reaching for the phone.

The guy on the doorstep was thin. Not weak-thin. Hard-thin. As if whatever burned inside of him burned too hot for fat to survive. He had blue eyes so pale they were almost gray. His silver hair was cropped tight to his skull, as was the goatee that clung to his lips and chin. It took Bob a second to recognize him—the kid who'd stuck his head in the bar five-six weeks back, asked if they served Zima.

The kid smiled and extended his hand. "Mr. Saginowski?"

Bob shook the hand. "Yes?"

"Bob Saginowski?" The man shook Bob's large hand with his small one, and there was a lot of power in the grip.

"Yeah?"

"Eric Deeds, Bob." The kid let go of his hand. "I believe you have my dog."

In the kitchen, Eric Deeds said, "Hey, there he is." He said, "That's my guy." He said, "He got big." He said, "The size of him."

Cassius slinked over to him, even climbed up on his lap when Eric, unbidden, took a seat at Bob's kitchen table and patted his inner thigh twice. Bob couldn't even say how it was Eric Deeds talked his way into the house; he was just one of those people had a way about him, like cops and Teamsters— he wanted in, he was coming in.

"Bob," Eric Deeds said, "I'm going to need him back." He had Cassius in his lap and was rubbing his belly. Bob felt a prick of envy as Cassius kicked his left leg, even though a constant shiver—almost a palsy—ran through his fur. Eric Deeds scratched under Cassius's chin. The dog kept his ears and tail pressed flat to his body. He looked ashamed, his eyes staring down into their sockets.

"Um . . ." Bob reached out and lifted Cassius off Eric's lap, plopped him down on his own, scratched behind his ears. "Cash is mine."

The act was between them now—Bob lifting the puppy off Eric's lap without any warning, Eric looking at him for just a second, like, The fuck was that all about? His forehead narrowed and it gave his eyes a surprised cast, as if they'd never expected to find themselves on his face. In that moment, he looked cruel, the kind of guy, if he was feeling sorry for himself, took a shit on the whole world.

"Cash?" he said.

Bob nodded as Cassius's ears unfurled from his head and he licked Bob's wrist. "Short for Cassius. That's his name. What did you call him?"

"Called him Dog mostly. Sometimes Hound."

Eric Deeds glanced around the kitchen, up at the old circular fluorescent in the ceiling, something going back to Bob's mother, hell, Bob's father just before the first stroke, around the time the old man had become obsessed with paneling—paneled the kitchen, the living room, the dining room, would've paneled the toilet if he could've figured out how.

Bob said, "You beat him."

Eric reached into his shirt pocket. He pulled out a cigarette and popped it in his mouth. He lit it, shook out the match, tossed it on Bob's kitchen table.

"You can't smoke in here."

Eric considered Bob with a level gaze and kept smoking. "I beat him?"

"Yeah."

"Uh, so what?" Eric flicked some ash on the floor. "I'm taking the dog, Bob."

Bob stood to his full height. He held tight to Cassius, who squirmed a bit in his arms and nipped at the flat of his hand. If it came to it, Bob decided, he'd drop all six feet three inches and two hundred ninety pounds of himself on Eric Deeds, who couldn't weigh more than a buck-seventy. Not now, not just standing there, but if Eric reached for Cassius, well then . . .

Eric Deeds blew a stream of smoke at the ceiling. "I saw you that night. I was feeling bad, you know, about my temper? So I went back to see if the hound was really dead or not and I watched you pluck him out of the trash."

"I really think you should go." Bob pulled his cell from his pocket and flipped it open. "I'm calling 911."

Eric nodded. "I've been in prison, Bob, mental hospitals. I've been a lotta places. I'll go again, don't mean a thing to me, though I doubt they'd prosecute even *me* for fucking up a *dog*. I mean, sooner or later, you gotta go to work or get some sleep."

"What is *wrong* with you?"

Eric held out of his hands. "Pretty much everything. And you took my dog."

"You tried to kill it."

Eric said, "Nah." Shook his head like he believed it.

"You can't have the dog."

"I need the dog."

"No."

"I love that dog."

"No."

"Ten thousand."

"What?"

Eric nodded. "I need ten grand. By tonight. That's the price."

Bob gave it a nervous chuckle. "Who has ten thousand dollars?"

"You could find it."

"How could I poss—"

"Say, that safe in Cousin Marv's office. You're a drop bar, Bob. You don't think half the neighborhood knows? So that might be a place to start."

Bob shook his head. "Can't be done. Any money we get during the day? Goes through a slot at the bar. Ends up in the office safe, yeah, but that's on a time—"

"—lock, I know." Eric turned on the couch, one arm stretched along the back of it. "Goes off at 2 a.m. in case they decide they need a last-minute payout for something who the fuck knows, but big. And you have ninety seconds to open and close it or it triggers two silent alarms, neither of which goes off in a police station or a security company. Fancy that." Eric took a hit off his cigarette. "I'm not greedy, Bob. I just need stake money for something. I don't want everything in the safe, just ten grand. You give me ten grand, I'll disappear."

"This is ludicrous."

"So, it's ludicrous."

"You don't just walk into someone's life and—"

"That *is* life: someone like me coming along when you're not looking."

Bob put Cassius on the floor but made sure he didn't wander over to the other side of the table. He needn't have worried—Cassius didn't move an inch, sat there like a cement post, eyes on Bob.

Eric Deeds said, "You're racing through all your options, but they're options for normal people in normal circumstances. I need my ten grand tonight. If you don't get it for me, I'll take your dog. *I* licensed him. You didn't, because you couldn't. Then I'll forget to feed him for a while. One day, when he gets all yappy about it, I'll beat his head in with a rock or something. Look in my eyes and tell me which part I'm lying about, Bob."

After he left, Bob went to his basement. He avoided it whenever he could, though the floor was white, as white as he'd been able to make it, whiter than it had ever been through most of its existence. He unlocked a cupboard over the old wash sink his father had often used after one of his adventures in paneling, and removed a yellow and brown Chock full o'Nuts can from the shelf. He pulled fifteen thousand from it. He put ten in his pocket and five back in the can. He looked around again at the white floor, at the black oil tank against the wall, at the bare bulbs.

Upstairs he gave Cassius a bunch of treats. He rubbed his ears and his belly. He assured the animal that he was worth ten thousand dollars.

Bob, three deep at the bar for a solid hour between 11 and midnight, looked through a sudden gap in the crowd and saw Eric sitting at the wobbly table under the Narragansett mirror. The Super Bowl was an hour over, but the crowd, drunk as shit, hung around. Eric had one arm stretched across the table and Bob followed it, saw that it connected to something. An arm. Nadia's arm. Nadia's face stared back at Eric, unreadable. Was she terrified? Or something else?

Bob, filling a glass with ice, felt like he was shoveling the cubes into his own chest, pouring them into his stomach and against the base of his spine. What did he know about Nadia, after all? He knew that he'd found a near-dead dog in the trash outside her house. He knew that Eric Deeds only came into his life after Bob had met her. He knew that her middle name, thus far, could be Lies of Omission.

When he was twenty-eight, Bob had come into his mother's bedroom to wake her for Sunday Mass. He'd given her a shake and she hadn't batted at his hand as she normally did. So he rolled her toward him and her face was scrunched tight, her eyes too, and her skin was curbstone-gray. Sometime in the night, after *Matlock* and the 10 o'clock news, she'd gone to bed and woke to God's fist clenched around her heart. Probably hadn't been enough air left in her lungs to cry out. Alone in the dark, clutching the sheets, that fist clenching, her face clenching, her eyes scrunching, the terrible knowledge dawning that, even for you, it all ends. And right now.

Standing over her that morning, imagining the last tick of her heart, the last lonely wish her brain had been able to form, Bob felt a loss unlike any he'd ever known or expected to know again.

Until tonight. Until now. Until he learned what that look on Nadia's face meant.

By 1:50, the crowd was gone, just Eric and Nadia and an old, stringent, functioning alcoholic named Millie who'd amble off to the assisted living place up on Pearl Street at 1:55 on the dot.

Eric, who had been coming to the bar for shots of Powers for the last hour, pushed back from the table and pulled Nadia across the floor with him. He sat her on a stool and Bob got a good look in her face finally, saw something he still couldn't fully identify—but it definitely wasn't excitement or smugness or the bitter smile of a victor. Maybe something worse than all of that—despair.

Eric gave him an all-teeth smile and spoke through it, softly. "When's the old biddie pack it in?"

"A couple minutes."

"Where's Marv?"

"I didn't call him in."

"Why not?"

"Someone's gonna take the blame for this, I figured it might as well be me."

"How noble of—"

"How do you know her?"

Eric looked over at Nadia hunched on the stool beside him. He leaned into the bar. "We grew up on the same block."

"He give you that scar?"

Nadia stared at him.

"Did he?"

"She gave herself the scar," Eric Deeds said.

"You did?" Bob asked her.

Nadia looked at the bar top. "I was pretty high."

"Bob," Eric said, "if you fuck with me—even in the slightest—it doesn't matter how long it takes me, I'll come back for her. And if you got any plans, like Eric-doesn't-walk-back-out-of-here plans? Not that you're that type of guy, but Marv might be? You got any ideas in that vein, Bob, my partner on the Richie Whalen hit, he'll take care of you both."

Eric sat back as mean old Millie left the same tip she'd been leaving since Sputnik—a quarter—and slid off her stool. She gave Bob a rasp that was ten percent vocal chords and ninety percent Virginia Slims Ultra Light 100s. "Yeah, I'm off."

"You take care, Millie."

She waved it away with a, "Yeah, yeah, yeah," and pushed open the door.

Bob locked it behind her and came back behind the bar. He wiped down the bar top. When he reached Eric's elbows, he said, "Excuse me."

"Go around."

Bob wiped the rag in a half-circle around Eric's elbows.

"Who's your partner?" Bob said.

"Wouldn't be much of a threat if you knew who he was, would he, Bob?"

"But he helped you kill Richie Whalen?"

Eric said, "That's the rumor, Bob."

"More than a rumor." Bob wiped in front of Nadia, saw red marks on her wrists where Eric had yanked them. He wondered if there were other marks he couldn't see.

"Well then it's more than a rumor, Bob. So there you go."

"There you go what?"

"There you *go*," Eric scowled. "What time is it, Bob?"

Bob placed ten thousand dollars on the bar. "You don't have to call me by my name all the time."

"I will see what I can do about that, Bob." Eric thumbed the bills. "What's this?"

"It's the ten grand you wanted for Cash."

Eric pursed his lips. "All the same, let's look in the safe."

"You sure?" Bob said. "I'm happy to buy him from you for ten grand."

"How much for Nadia, though?"

"Oh."

"Yeah. Oh."

Bob thought about that new wrinkle for a bit and poured himself a closing-time shot of vodka. He raised it to Eric Deeds and then drank it down. "You know, Marv used to have a problem with blow about ten years ago?"

"I did not know that, Bob."

Bob shrugged, poured them all a shot of vodka. "Yeah, Marv liked the coke too much but it didn't like him back."

Eric drank Nadia's shot. "Getting close to 2 here, Bob."

"He was more of a loan shark then. I mean, he did some fence, but mostly he was a shark. There was this kid? Into Marv for a shitload of money. Real hopeless case when it came to the dogs and basketball. Kinda kid could never pay back all he owed."

Eric drank his own shot. "One fifty-seven, Bob."

"The thing, though? This kid, he actually hit on a slot at Mohegan. Hit for twenty-two grand. Which is just a little more than he owed Marv."

"And he didn't pay Marv back, so you and Marv got all hard on him and I'm supposed to learn—"

"No, no. He *paid* Marv. Paid him every cent. What the kid didn't know, though, was that Marv had been skimming. Because of the coke habit? And this kid's money was like manna from heaven as long as no one knew it was from this kid. See what I'm saying?"

"Bob, it's fucking one minute to 2." Sweat on Eric's lip.

"Do you see what I'm saying?" Bob asked. "Do you understand the story?"

Eric looked to the door to make sure it was locked. "Fine, yeah. This kid, he had to be ripped off."

"He had to be killed."

Out of the side of his eye, a quick glance. "Okay, killed."

Bob could feel Nadia's eyes lock on him suddenly, her head cock a bit. "That way, he couldn't ever say he paid off Marv and no one else could either. Marv uses the money to cover all the holes, he cleans up his act, it's like it never happened. So that's what we did."

"You did . . ." Eric barely in the conversation, but some warning in his head starting to sound, his head turning from the clock toward Bob.

"Killed him in my basement," Bob said. "Know what his name was?"

"I wouldn't know, Bob."

"Sure you would. Richie Whelan."

Bob reached under the bar and pulled out the 9mm. He didn't notice the safety was on, so when he pulled the trigger nothing happened. Eric jerked his head and pushed back from the bar rail, but Bob thumbed off the safety and shot Eric just below the throat. The gunshot sounded like aluminum siding being torn off a house. Nadia screamed. Not a long scream, but sharp with shock. Eric made a racket falling back off his stool, and by the time Bob came around the bar, Eric was already going, if not quite gone. The overhead fan cast thin slices of shadow over his face. His cheeks puffed in and out like he was trying to catch his breath and kiss somebody at the same time.

"I'm sorry, but you kids," Bob said. "You know? You go out of the house dressed like you're still in your living room. You say terrible things about women. You hurt harmless dogs. I'm tired of you, man."

Eric stared up at him. Winced like he had heartburn. He looked pissed off. Frustrated. The expression froze on his face like it was sewn there, and then he wasn't in his body anymore. Just gone. Just, shit, dead.

Bob dragged him into the cooler.

When he came back, pushing the mop and bucket ahead of him, Nadia still sat on her stool. Her mouth was a bit wider than usual and she couldn't take her eyes off the floor where the blood was, but otherwise she seemed perfectly normal.

"He would have just kept coming," Bob said. "Once someone takes something from you and you let them? They don't feel gratitude, they just feel like you owe them more." He soaked the mop in the bucket, wrung it out a bit, and slopped it over the main blood spot. "Makes no sense, right? But that's how they feel. Entitled. And you can never change their minds after that."

She said, "He . . . You just fucking shot him. You just . . . I mean, you know?"

Bob swirled the mop over the spot. "He beat my dog."

The Chechens took care of the body after a discussion with the Italians and the Micks. Bob was told his money was no good at several restaurants for the next couple of months, and they gave him four tickets to a Celtics game. Not floor seats, but pretty good ones.

Bob never mentioned Nadia. Just said Eric showed up at the end of the evening, waved a gun around, said to take him to the office safe. Bob let him do his ranting, do his waving, found an opportunity, and shot him. And that was it. End of Eric, end of story.

Nadia came to him a few days later. Bob opened the door and she stood there on his stoop with a bright winter day turning everything sharp and clear behind her. She held up a bag of dog treats.

"Peanut butter," she said, her smile bright, her eyes just a little wet. "With a hint of molasses."

Bob opened the door wide and stepped back to let her in.

"I've gotta believe," Nadia said, "there's a purpose. And even if it's that you kill me as soon as I close my eyes—"

"Me? What? No," Bob said. "Oh, no."

"—then that's okay. Because I just can't go through any more of this alone. Not another day."

"Me too." He closed his eyes. "Me too."

They didn't speak for a long time. He opened his eyes, peered at the ceiling of his bedroom. "Why?"

"Hmm?"

"This. You. Why are you with me?"

She ran a hand over his chest and it gave him a shiver. In his whole life, he never would have expected to feel a touch like that on his bare skin.

"Because I like you. Because you're nice to Cassius."

"And because you're scared of me?"

"I dunno. Maybe. But more the other reason."

He couldn't tell if she was lying. Who could tell when anyone was? Really. Every day, you ran into people and half of them, if not more, could be lying to you. Why?

Why not?

You couldn't tell who was true and who was not. If you could, lie detectors would never have been invented. Someone stared in your face and said, *I'm telling the truth.* They said, *I promise.* They said, *I love you.*

And you were going to say what to that? Prove it?

"He needs a walk."

"Huh?"

"Cassius. He hasn't been out all day."

"I'll get the leash."

In the park, the February sky hung above them like a canvas tarp. The weather had been almost mild for a few days. The ice had broken on the river but small chunks of it clung to the dark banks.

He didn't know what he believed. Cassius walked ahead of them, pulling on the leash a bit, so proud, so pleased, un-recognizable from the quivering hunk of fur Bob had pulled from a barrel just two and a half months ago.

Two and a half months! Wow. Things sure could change in a hurry. You rolled over one morning, and it was a whole new world. It turned itself toward the sun, stretched and yawned. It turned itself toward the night. A few more hours, turned itself toward the sun again. A new world, every day.

When they reached the center of the park, he unhooked the leash from Cassius's collar and reached into his coat for a tennis ball. Cassius reared his head. He snorted loud. He pawed the earth. Bob threw the ball and the dog took off after it. Bob envisioned the ball taking a bad bounce into the road. The screech of tires, the thump of metal against dog. Or what would happen if Cassius, suddenly free, just kept running.

But what could you do?

You couldn't control things.

THE PLACE WHERE HE BELONGS

BY JIM FUSILLI

Beacon Hill

After nearly twenty years at the United Nations, his wife was offered a position with Harvard's Kennedy School of Government, and she was thrilled. He was not. "Jeff, are you sure you'll be all right leaving here?" she asked. What could he say? A fair-minded man would acknowledge she'd sacrificed for his career.

During the first week in town, they were invited to a cocktail party in Cambridge. "How long had you lived in New York?" inquired one of her new colleagues.

"Forty-nine years," he replied.

"And you are . . . ?"

"Forty-nine," he said, scratching his two-day growth.

"Oh my goodness," said the man's wife, "I wonder what you'll make of us."

When they were leaving, the host called him Joe.

They settled over by the Museum of Science, and he explored the music clubs—the Dise and T.T. the Bear's, mostly. He went to shows at the Orpheum, where he had opened for Jesse Colin Young long ago, and concerts at the colleges and at Berklee, roaming by himself while Maya prepared for her lectures. A few musicians he worked with in the '80s played the Garden, and he walked over, hunched and shivering in a biting wind as he crossed the Charles. Backstage, hugs all around and "What are you up to?" "You know," he shrugged.

He called Club Passim and asked if he could do a set or two. Thank you, no.

Soon Maya said they were better suited to Beacon Hill, near where several of her colleagues lived, and she found a condo on Beacon Street, two floors in a brownstone built in 1848, the former French consulate, reasonably priced by Manhattan standards, an investment in a down market, and with space for his music room. "Your call," he said, since he'd made only $6,200 in royalties in the previous year.

She said that she felt revitalized by the new city, that Harvard was a miracle of intelligence and discourse. She was learning, and having fun. He noticed that she no longer asked if he wanted to go back to New York. Boston was becoming her home, while he felt he'd been exiled.

With little else to do, he soundproofed an upstairs bedroom and brought in his equipment—his upright piano, his guitars, a classic Fender bass, his old reel-to-reel tape recorder, mikes and stands, cables, and silver tape. He put baffle over the windows, his old Persian rug on the floor. His platinum album went downstairs in the living room. The label had sent one to every songwriter who contributed to the Grammy-winning soundtrack album. His tender love song was performed at weddings, and even people with little interest in pop music knew the words he'd written. This went on for years, the money rolling in. Then a comedian did a version on *Letterman*, mugging it up as he serenaded a pig in a straw bonnet. No one took the song seriously from then on. You couldn't listen to the original version without thinking of the comedian, his rubbery face, squealing voice, and the damned pig. In time, his publisher dropped him. Who'd sing any tune written by a man whose music was so easily ridiculed? Fortunately, they'd set aside enough money for their son to finish at Stanford. His wife had preached frugality even in his best years: before the chaos of his sudden acclaim, they'd planned on having more children. They tried even when it seemed too late.

Beacon Hill was unbearable. He couldn't find its rhythm, couldn't recognize the cues. He was out of place, and nothing he did made him feel any better. Daily life was a relentless series of insults and indignities. People were smug and complacent. Common courtesy didn't exist. No one said hello or thank you or held open a door. His wife, a temperate soul, couldn't disagree completely when he said there was something odd and off-putting about the place. A cleaner on Charles Street misplaced two of her suits for nine days and never apologized. She'd ordered a case of wine for a party at their apartment and it never arrived. "Service isn't a priority," she concluded. He couldn't find plantains at the grocer's, and the bagels sucked. No one knew what he'd done.

She loved her job, and called the neighborhood a walker's delight—the town houses, antique shops, Acorn Street, the esplanade on the Charles, the way the sun shone when spring finally arrived. She took his arm as they crossed the Salt-and-Pepper Bridge, sailboats gliding below.

After Maya went to bed, he'd walk across to the Public Garden, his guitar and case in hand, hoping something would come to him. In Washington Square Park, he'd have drawn a crowd. Here, nobody cared. During the day, he'd slip into a T-shirt, tug on jeans, and bring a sandwich to a bench where he'd watch swans drift on the lake; nearby were flowers and nannies with cheery babies running on chubby legs. He'd smile, nod, but no one responded. In New York, he'd meet friends for lunch. He'd see people on the street. Everybody was open and welcoming. *Hey, Jeff!* they'd shout. Here, there was no refuge, no place to hide. He was a balloon drifting toward the high, boundless sky.

Staring at his platinum album, he saw his gaunt, ghostly reflection and was surprised to find he was still there.

"Did you hear about the baby?" Maya said, as she hung up her skirt.

He shook his head. "I didn't go out."

She was going to ask if he heard it on the radio, but he'd become completely disengaged. He'd even stopped streaming WNYC. "A baby is missing. Stolen."

She came to him with a flier she'd been given at the Charles Street T station. It said the baby was taken in the Public Garden yesterday. She had been sitting in a stroller over by the *Make Way for Ducklings* statue. So many children were laughing and playing. One fell and cut a knee on the cobblestone. When a nanny rushed over to help, leaving the infant's stroller for a moment . . .

"You could jump into a car and be on 90 to New York in five minutes," he said.

"They're looking for people who were in the park to help."

"Good luck." He had it in his mind Beacon Hill wouldn't piss on somebody if he was on fire. He didn't believe her when she said it wasn't Beacon Hill's fault, reminding him that he'd struggled for the past few years in New York.

He went to his studio while she made dinner—salmon and a cold rice dish she'd picked up on Charles Street. When he came down, she was pouring Pinot Grigio as she read a working paper on the Fair Trade movement.

After they ate, he brought the dishes to the sink. Soon soap bubbles rose and popped.

"Jeff. Are you coming?"

He grabbed a towel. "Where?"

"To the vigil, remember? Everybody's helping with the baby."

"These people?"

"Stop it," she said. "I'm going. I wish you would."

"I've got work," he told her. "I'll be upstairs."

After he brought the trash to the basement, he walked outside and stood on the steps. Over in the Public Garden, hundreds of people were fanned out, studying the grass and grounds, looking into the tulip beds, hoping for a clue, any tidbit of information, a revelation. Klieg lights police had stationed on the pathways shed an eerie glow throughout the park, and there were long, quivering shadows. Kids in shorts and hoodies served cold drinks. An uncomfortable silence and an unsettling sense of dread filled the early summer air.

Maya was over by the *Angel of the Waters*, the statue that reminded him of one with the same name in Central Park, and she was chatting with a thick, busty blonde. As the other woman lectured, Maya folded her arms, solemnity on her face. When she spotted him, she beckoned him with a wave, but he pointed upstairs and made a little gesture like he was strumming a guitar. Then he went back inside.

"I'm onto something," he said when she returned. "Don't be surprised if I don't come to bed." He held up a cloth sack she'd gotten at the Museum of Fine Arts that he'd filled with snacks and something to drink.

"Jeff," she said, as she kicked off her flats, "look at this."

Another flier. A sketch by a police artist.

"It looks like you, Jeff."

"No, it doesn't," he said, as he nudged it back toward her.

"Gail McDermott thought so."

"Gail McDermott . . . ?"

"The blonde on the first floor . . . Runs a PR agency . . ."

He didn't know anyone in the building. "No," he said, tapping the flier, "that guy is old. He's half bald. Scruffy. It's not me."

"I didn't say it *was* you . . ."

"I'm going upstairs."

"They're going to drag the lake tomorrow," she told him.

Walking away, he said, "She's not dead."

He couldn't keep the baby in his music room. It was as dark as a cave, and the soundproofing left the air stagnant and stale. He'd changed her and fed her and burped her and held her, tickled her chin, combed her downy hair with his fingers, bathed her with warm water with a face cloth, cooed at her, sang to her, played little figures on the piano. But the carton he converted to a bassinet was stupid, and she needed sunlight, so he brought her downstairs into the kitchen and sat with her on his lap by Maya's basil plants and thyme leaves.

"Hey baby," he said as he cuddled her in his arms.

Out on Beacon Hill, people had pulled their chins out of the air and were treating each other with decency and humility. They had a cause bigger than themselves now, something beyond parading their imaginary status. Or so he assumed. He hadn't left the apartment grounds since he took Baby Alice. Remembering that a few residents in the building didn't retrieve their *Globe* until the day's end, he brought her to the center of the king-sized bed, nestled her on goose down, and took the creaking spiral staircase to the lobby. As he started back up, the *Globe* under his hand, he heard the baby cry and hurried back to scoop her in his arms. He said, "It's all right, baby. Everything's all right." He bounced her and rubbed her back until she sighed and stopped fussing. He kissed her moist cheek.

Down in her office in apartment 3, statue-still and silent, sat Gail McDermott, who, though she tried, couldn't convince herself she hadn't heard a baby's cry. Fresh cup of coffee in hand, she lifted the flier with the police sketch from her in-box, and yeah, it did look like Maya's husband, that New Yorker who was some sort of musician, the odd, scowling guy who dressed like a teenager and looked like he needed something no one could provide.

"Jim," she called as she knocked again. "Jim."

He opened the door a crack. "It's Jeff," he said.

"Jeff." Gail McDermott introduced herself by handing him a business card. "I heard a baby."

"Not here." He scanned the card. *McDermott Communications*, it read. *Specialists in Crisis Management*. The building's address was printed below.

"Do you have the baby?"

"Do I have—"

McDermott pushed in, and he watched as she surveyed the living room. Plain, plump, and round-faced, she wore business slacks and a snug white silk blouse. No makeup, her hair tucked behind her ears. Flip-flops and a PDA on her belt.

"No baby here," Jeff said, standing by the door.

"I could've sworn— What's this?" She stared at the platinum album, framed on the wall. "I love this movie. Wait— You wrote this song? *That* song?"

The one with the pig, he thought, *yeah*.

"That was my sister's wedding song." She turned. "That's a beautiful song. Wicked beautiful."

"Thank—"

Upstairs, Baby Alice let out a cry. He sank as he realized he'd left the door open to his soundproof studio.

"Oh, Jeff . . ." McDermott said, puffing up.

Maya and Jeff, the baby in his lap, faced McDermott, who sat behind her desk, the *Angel of the Waters* in the Public Garden over her shoulder. Like Jeff, she'd converted a bedroom to a workspace.

"Why?" Maya repeated.

He said, "I don't know why."

"Was she in danger, Jeff?" McDermott asked.

"No. She was asleep."

"Tell me what you were thinking . . ."

He shrugged. "I wasn't thinking. I just, I don't know, reacted."

"To what?" Maya asked.

Is a man who no longer matters supposed to understand why he did something? "I don't know. Really," he replied truthfully. He looked down at the baby, who slept peacefully. *Here, Maya*, he wanted to say. *I'm sorry. Take her and let's go home.*

But it was more, and much less, than that.

"Ever do anything like this before?" McDermott asked.

"No. Of course not."

"We need a lawyer," Maya said.

"I'll get you one," McDermott replied, holding up a blunt index finger. "But let's think this through . . ."

She'd wriggled politicians, businessmen, and academics out of worse situations than this. Had the Patriots listened to her, the nation wouldn't think of them as cheaters. Had Larry Summers, he'd still be president of Harvard.

She rubbed her temples. Stealing a baby from a stroller could seem a low thing. It had to be spun right. The guilty party had to define the crime.

"It was an impulse," Jeff said.

"So this is what you do in New York? You have an impulse and you steal a baby?"

He hung his head.

"Have you called the police?" Maya asked. She was still stunned, the morning a blur since she was pulled from the lecture hall.

"That's not at the top of our agenda," McDermott replied. "We have to inculcate Jeff here."

"Are you saying we sneak the baby back into the park?" Maya asked.

"We could do that," McDermott replied. "But how does that help him?"

Maya frowned. "For one, he may stay out of jail . . ."

"That's the minimum outcome," McDermott said as she stood. "We can do better than that."

Jeff brushed the baby's hair from her forehead.

"Why does he take her?" McDermott said as she started to pace. "He's distressed, his career in shambles, no one acknowledges him. He has a sort of psychotic breakdown. Do I have that right, Jeff?"

"Just about," he admitted.

Maya looked at her husband, surprised he'd said it aloud.

"Or he's committed an act of civic disobedience against Beacon Hill. He feels a smugness, a starchiness, a lack of soul . . . He's worried the child will grow up with a distorted sense of self. She'll be ill-equipped for life outside a tiny, out-of-touch neighborhood in a dynamic city, a great nation."

Maya turned as McDermott circled behind her. "You don't believe that, do you?" she asked.

"There's less pretension on Rodeo Drive," answered Mc-Dermott, who had grown up in the Ninth Street Projects.

"No, I meant you can't believe the police will accept that as an explanation."

"The police will be easy," McDermott said. "Getting your husband back on top of the music business is the trick."

"I never was on top, actually." Jeff stared at Baby Alice. He wondered what their daughter might've looked like if ambition hadn't gotten between his word and Maya and their son.

"Go shower and shave, Jeff," McDermott said, as she returned to her desk. "Maya, get over to Newbury Street and buy him some grown-up clothes. I'll watch the baby." As she sat, she added, "By the way, I get five hundred dollars an hour, and you're on the clock until this is done."

Okay then. Two in the morning and Jeff was in his spot, his guitar on his lap, his fingers on the steel strings. The *Angel of the Waters* hovered over him, wings open, arms outstretched. Cast as far as he could see, the park was splendid under a starry summer sky, the flowers asleep until dawn. In the near distance, a policeman patrolled on horseback.

He strummed a minor chord, another, anoth—

What? Was that . . . Was that a baby's cry?

He put the guitar on its case, walked to the dry, shallow fountain at the foot of the statue, and, oh my God, there was a baby. The missing baby. Baby Alice.

He scooped her up, nestled her in his arms, and dashed to Beacon Street. There wasn't a car in sight. Damn. Plan B.

He raced to their building and rang every bell. Someone answered, a man with a high, flowery voice.

"I found the baby," Jeff said hurriedly into the speaker. "The missing baby. I found it. Call the police."

McDermott, in plaid pajama bottoms and a Big Papi T-shirt, reached him first, and by the time Maya rushed downstairs in her robe and slippers, most of the building was in the lobby, waving at the baby, patting Jeff on the back.

"Look, Maya," he said breathlessly. "She was in the park. Under the statue."

"It's a miracle," she muttered.

"She doesn't look hurt," McDermott said, peering over Maya's shoulder.

Jeff nodded. He was crisp in new green khakis, a striped shirt from Brooks Brothers, and boating shoes, his hair combed, the part where it should be. For a moment, he drifted deep into the story McDermott had concocted. He felt like a man who'd done something worthwhile.

Wanting no part of the charade, Maya left to retrieve his guitar.

The police came. Two squad cars, burly guys in uniforms. The *Herald* beat the *Globe* there, and its photographer got him cradling the baby, cops surrounding them as they came down the brownstone steps. "Sox Sweep Yanks—Again!" read the *Herald* headline that ran alongside a vertical photo of Jeff and Baby Alice. "Our Angel Safe and Sound" was the caption. The story on page three identified him as a famous Hollywood songwriter. They got his first name right, all four letters, and found an old photo of him sandwiched between Linda Ronstadt and Bonnie Raitt taken at some benefit show long ago.

"That was an awful thing to do, Jeffrey," Maya said, turning away whenever he approached. "You need help."

Citizens Bank tried to give him the $5,000 reward they'd put up, but, as McDermott instructed, he insisted it go to Baby Alice. Her parents, cordial young lawyers who were saving to buy their first home, thanked Jeff by inviting him and Maya to brunch on Rowes Wharf. Over the meal, he learned the nanny was back in Nicaragua, courtesy of immigration services.

"Glad you got that poor woman deported?" Maya asked as they walked back to their apartment.

He was glad about a lot of things, if not that. The day after the baby was recovered, Jeff was flown to New York to appear on *The Early Show*, where he was interviewed about the Miracle of the Angel.

"Yes, I have some new songs," he said as the interview wound down.

"Will you be writing one about Baby Alice?"

"I like that idea," he replied, as McDermott had instructed when she media-trained him.

Some big country music star he'd never heard of asked to hear his new material. A publisher with offices in New York, Nashville, Los Angeles, and London offered to rep him. And a hip-hop mega-producer secured the rights to his old song from the movie, pledging to turn it into a hit again, "as soon as I find the look for the product."

When he finally returned to Beacon Hill, he hardly recognized the woman who greeted him. Despite the turmoil, Maya seemed content, energized yet at ease, all the sharp angles gone. The pace of the old town suited her, she said. She'd moved on. "Go back to New York, Jeff," she said, and he did.

DARK WATERS

BY PATRICIA POWELL

Watertown

Promptly at 7:19, right in the middle of *Jeopardy!*, the entire house went black; no electricity! and she'd had to rustle through her drawers to find candles to light up the kitchen so she could see to eat a tin of sardines with crackers and slog through half a bottle of Chardonnay. Later she had crept upstairs, weary and slightly depressed, to read peacefully a book on uncertainty she'd been trying to sink her teeth into for some time. She had not long settled into the chapter on "discomfort" when she heard the knocking on the front door downstairs, which was immediately perplexing for she did not really know anyone in the area that intimately, she'd just moved near six months now, had told no one of her whereabouts except her best friend Rhonda, and she was not expecting Rhonda, nor expecting that Rhonda would've disclosed her location to Fred. And yet who could it be knocking on her door at this hour—11 according to the clock on the bedside table. Who could it be?

She swung out of bed irritated as hell, padded over to the window, and flung back the lace curtains. Outside the night was impenetrable and the trees swayed drunkenly and against the frosted window, the silvery slanted rain. It had been raining all day, and now it was dark, with big winds howling through the walls and the rain battering the roof, and outside, outside was the black and sodden night. She was wearing a long see-through pink gown that in the early years of her marriage used to excite her husband greatly. But that was another story altogether. She hauled on a white duster over her gown, pulled on satin slippers, and looked around quickly for something big, something heavy, something that with just one blow would carry off the culprit. She found a screwdriver, which she slipped into her pocket, and a big heavy-duty metal flashlight she switched on at once, lighting her way downstairs to put an end to the disturbance.

Her name was Perle, she was forty-seven, and just six months ago she got up one morning and decided she was leaving her marriage. She was not leaving her children, mind you, who were away at college, she was leaving Fred, as things between them had been dead for some time, the two of them like ships passing in the night en route to some unknown destination. The truth was, early on she had lost herself, had given it over, thinking that was love, did not know where he ended and she began, and now she wanted to retrieve herself, for she had stopped living, she was just coasting now, on the sea of life. It sounded like a cliché, she knew, but that was how she saw it. She did not say a word to him the morning she left. She waited until he was gone to the hospital to visit the sick and the dying—he was an evangelical minister who believed in the laying on of hands—then she packed one suitcase full of clothes, another of her face products as she had a tendency to break out into boils, and she called the movers to collect the upright her mother had given her. Heading west, she slowly drove away from her life that morning in the white Pontiac, stopping only once to fill it with gas and to buy a cheese sandwich and a bottle of water. She rented a semi-furnished one-bedroom in Watertown, a sleepy little place that had a river running through it. She knew no one, no one knew her, and except for the tortured sonatas she played in the early mornings upon arising, she interacted only with the hairdresser where she went for a weekly rinse and set, the cashier at the bank for she was living off some CDs she'd put away for a rainy day, and the Armenian grocers that lined both sides of the main drag with their dark overstocked little shops full of Mediterranean goods.

Who is it? she cried weakly, and then she muscled up herself, for this was ridiculous. Who is it? she snapped, her voice unrecognizable even to her, and the pounding stopped at once. A face was pressed up against the glass, a dark face wet and wild with a falling-down mustache and a felt hat pulled so low she could barely see the eyes, but she could sense the desperateness in them. And when a sliver of lightning lit up the porch, she saw it was a white man slightly stooped, or maybe he was holding something, his raincoat glowing in the brief light.

It was crazy what she was about to do, she knew all the stories, knew them up and down, knew too there were white men who preyed on black women, and yet she yanked open the door and he stumbled in, wet and heavy and dank with the smell of dread.

What? she cried. What's the matter! She ushered him into the kitchen, where he leaked water all over her floor, perhaps even blood, she could smell iron. She had the light pointed on his face, which looked gray and swollen, and on his pin-striped suit, on the untied shoes that looked slightly small for his long slim frame. She had the screwdriver poised for his heart at her side.

Help me, he gasped, leaning on the kitchen counter, and holding his arm that looked unhinged. They've shot me.

Blood was seeping onto her clean white Formica table and collecting into black pools.

She did not ask who had shot him; she did not want to know. She lit the candles on the counter, grabbed the light, and flew upstairs, pulling out towels and antiseptic fluids and ammonia and bandages and gauze, a pair of scissors, tweezers, pliers, and pain relievers, whatever she could find. She had a well-stocked medicine cabinet.

Downstairs he had removed the jacket, and his shirt was soaked with blood and the blood was still dripping on the floor she had just mopped that morning and he was whimpering like something half dead. Should I call an ambulance? she asked him. Should I call the police? Take you to the hospital. She tried to remember where she'd seen one.

And he turned to look at her, perhaps for the first time, and the hardness on his face disquieted her. I wouldn't do that if I were you, he said coolly.

A fat piece of rage flew into her chest suddenly. Was he threatening her, was this fucker threatening her in her own house after she had dragged him in, that piece of shit? She let the rage hang there between them for a minute. Finally she said, Well, just so you know, mister, you can't stay here, okay, you can't fucking stay here. She was out of breath, winded. She could see the phone and she tried to think who she could call if this joker tried to play the fool. She'd rented the house from an older lesbian couple who were psychiatrists and who lived two houses down with their adopted son Ron, who they said had Attention Deficit Hyperactive Disorder, but that term, she'd come to learn, was just a euphemism for crabby and rude and antisocial behavior. She could call them. Or, if she screamed, there was George the electrician across the street, she'd met him just yesterday, and there was the woman to her right whose dog was always shitting in her yard; there was the old geezer on the other side who leered at all the young women who passed his porch. Chuck. But even if she screamed, who would hear her with all this rain battering down?

Help me, he whimpered like a half-dead dog, help me clean this up, please. He was losing massive amounts of blood, she could see that now, and his face looked scared and at the same time slightly suprised. His full lips were loose and leaking.

She could just let him bleed to death, she was thinking. But she was not that kind of person. She didn't think she could do that. Here, she said, dropping some pills into his hand that shook mightily and giving him a glass of juice. He swallowed them quickly, his Adam's apple sliding up and down. Then she set to work, boiling water on the gas stove, helping him out of his shirt that smelled like shit and sulphite, hauling him over to the sink where she proceeded to extract the bullet with her assortment of instruments, and to bathe and dress and bandage the wound. She was good at this; she'd been an emergency room nurse until a few years ago. She was gentle and patient, as she tended to be with all things maimed. The whimpering soon subsided. She could see he was impressed, but more than that, relieved. Perhaps even grateful. He could have bled to death or the wound could've turned septic. It took a good thirty minutes, and during that time she felt his eyes moving up and down her chest—she was stacked—and around her neck and arms which were strong and scented with ginger and musk oil.

Have you eaten? she asked him.

He nodded wearily. And she saw that he was not a bad-looking man, his face was bony and square, his eyes big and long-lashed, and he wore his hair cut close and even to his head. The mustache made him look older than he probably was; she put him to be slightly past fifty. He was not a very big man; she could take him down, she decided, if it came to that, she was strong. Still, he was muscle-bound, as if he'd spent a lot of time in jail or at the gym. She did not think it was the latter. He wore a layer of defeat about him that reminded her of Russell.

You have family around here? she asked him. You married? She made her voice hard.

Twice, he said. Two kids. One at community college. The girl. You?

She shook her head and remembered that she was wearing her duster—and underneath that her pink gown—and she pulled the string tighter around her waist and pressed down her hair, which felt big and heavy suddenly. Did she have toothpaste on her face? Sometimes she used toothpaste to stop the swelling boils. Her fingers edged up toward her cheeks to check. She breathed in relief.

Divorced, she said when she saw that his eyes were still moving on her honey skin, and then she could've kicked herself. My boyfriend should be coming home about now, she added, and glanced at the clock on the wall, which had stopped at 7:19.

Got in with the wrong crowd, he said, as if he hadn't heard that her man was coming home. And now they're on my ass.

Coke. She said this softly. She didn't even know why she said it. But he seemed like he'd do it big. He looked the kind who would want to impress.

He sighed without answering. Then: They think I have the money.

She nodded.

I ditched the car and then hoofed it. Fuckers shot me.

She didn't look at him, she didn't want to encourage him;

she didn't want details. Here was another boy playing at being a man. She knew that crowd. Did he even ask his wife about the cocaine, did he even say to her, Look, love, things piling up, I have this plan? Did he even allow her to talk him out of it? How about this, she might have said, instead? No, he had a scheme, some get-rich-quick scheme, some half-baked idea with a bunch of criminals. But everyone wants to be the hero. Russell too wanted to be a hero. She thought his mustache was ridiculous. He didn't earn it.

She was exhausted. It was late. She had wiped up the blood from off the floor and the counter and disposed of the rags and the bullet. She was ready for him to go now so she could get back to her life. Except he didn't look like someone ready to move. She grabbed two glasses from the cabinet and a bottle of Jack Daniel's. She poured him a finger, which he sucked down at once; she poured him another and one for herself, which she sipped slowly there at the kitchen table, the rain coming down outside, the flickering candles between them, the light low and soft on their drugged and morbid faces, their shadows skittering off the walls.

She missed Fred something furious; she had not missed him all this time—but tonight suddenly she wanted his taste on her tongue, his long dark neck, his beautiful mouth with the lips shaped like a heart, his breath jagged and harsh. She imagined him picking up the phone, his surprise at first, which he would immediately cover up by hardening his voice. Then it would be like pulling teeth trying to get anything out of him, anything warm. It was close to 12:30, by this time he'd be asleep or perhaps reading still and sipping the glass of port he took at night before bed, his feet covered in socks no matter how warm the night; it helped him sleep, he said. And what would she tell him? She'd let a white man into her house.

A man who could kill her. A man she did not know from Adam.

She found another candle, lit it, and gave it to him.

The bathroom is upstairs to the left, she said, you'll find towels too, and soap.

She turned away from his eyes like coals in the night, and busied herself in the kitchen as he trailed away with the light and started heavily up the stairs. She heard the door close, heard him tinkling, heard the toilet flush, and now the tub was filling with water.

She had to call somebody, needed to call somebody. But when she picked up the phone and put it to her ear, she saw that it was dead and that the line was cut.

Motherfucker! she thundered up at him, the panic eating at her now. Where was her cell, where the fuck was her cell? She scrambled around in the dark, knocking over bottles, crashing into bins; a glass fell on the floor and shattered. Jesus Christ! The terror was at her throat. She couldn't find her purse. She couldn't find her keys. She couldn't find anything at all. She turned Jack Daniel's to her head, gulped down a mouthful, and when that didn't produce the desired result, she swiftly swallowed several more. Fred's favorite sermon was about evil. You had to defeat it, he said. You can never let the seeds of it flourish. It is like cancer, he liked to tell the crowd, the worst, most virulent form, it spreads like wild fire. And when she'd tried to follow his reasoning about what this evil was, it was always the unknown, it was the surprise, and it was the challenge, the unpredictability. He was a careful man, that Fred. She'd left because of her faith, or maybe her lack of it. She didn't have conviction. She didn't have belief. She didn't have strong boundaries against evil, and how could she when she was always so curious about the unknown?

Suddenly there were footsteps thudding up the stairs at the front of the house. There were voices out there, men talking, there was banging on the front door again, banging on the glass, and she stood up with a start, her heart pounding again. This time the bell was ringing too, and she sat down and got up again, she heard sirens wailing outside, and whirling lights filled the room. It was the police. She ran to the door with the candle; she flung it open wide with a wild and certain joy.

Officer?

He was young and fat, his cheeks like apples.

Ma'am? He sounded surprised to see her. Maybe it was because she was black, or because she was in her duster, with her hair unsuppressed about her face. Ma'am, he said again, sorry to bother you.

Her face must've looked weary at this point. And she was weary.

Ma'am. He thrust a picture in her face. Ma'am, this man is very dangerous. Just escaped from Walpole. Maximum security. We're going around the neighborhood looking for him. We have the stolen car outside, so we know he isn't far. Have you seen anyone?

She felt faint suddenly. She remembered when they came for Russell, fifteen of them for one little nineteen-year-old boy. She must've rocked unsteadily, for the officer caught her under the arms.

You're okay, ma'am?

She opened her mouth to speak, to tell them that the piece of shit they were looking for was upstairs now in her tub, naked as the day he was born, that she'd patched him up, patched up the arm nice and good and extracted the bullet, and how did he thank her, he cut the telephone wire, that's what he did, he cut the wire. And despite herself, despite herself, she yawned loud and staggering. Then she yawned again and again, as if her brain needed an extraordinary amount of oxygen.

Sorry to wake you, ma'am. It's just that the stolen car is right outside.

She paused to peer into the night but all she saw were the circling lights from the police cars and Russell spread-eagle, fifteen guns pointed at his head. And then, in the distance, George's house, and faces pressed against the windows watching.

Look, ma'am, if anyone comes by asking for help, do not let him in, do you hear me? We might have shot him, and he might be bleeding. In fact, call us at once, call 911. I'm Officer Derrick. Tom Derrick. He took her hand, which was limp and slightly damp. Sorry to bother you like this. He was about to walk away and then he reconsidered.

Ma'am, we're just going to take a look around the back; make sure you're safe. Then we're going to check next door. Thanks again for your time.

She watched them traipse down the stairs, must be about six of them. She watched them fan out, turning the corner to the side of the house, shining their big lights. She heard them unlock the gate and step across the garden, their shoes sluicing through mud. She could hear them banging on the door of the woman next door whose dog often shat in her yard. She could hear them rooting around for some time before they slammed back into their cars and drove away. She looked out at the everlasting falling rain and at the streak of white light zigzagging the sky from the west. She waited for the thunderclap to blast through the heavens. And then she cleared her throat to make sure her voice box was still in operation. Hello, she cried into the night so she could hear herself. Hello! The air felt good on her skin; in fact, it was warmer outside than it was inside her house, which was freezing.

She turned back to her house, locked the door behind her, and leaned against it; a sigh sounding like a wail heaved out of her chest.

Fucking pigs!

She reeled at the sound of his voice so near her neck and ran smack into him, his chest like steel against her duster, which had flown open. She screamed then, and immediately caught herself and whacked him hard across the face with the flashlight. He cried out. She whacked again and again until he found her wrists and grabbed them. He thrust her against the wall, his breath acrid against her neck. And for a long time they stayed in that dance. She could tell he was thinking, thinking what exactly to do with her. He could not read her motives.

Cool it! he barked, his nails biting into her flesh. Don't get crazy now, okay, bitch? Don't get fucking crazy.

She could not see his eyes, but she imagined they were small and mean, the eyes of a man who could kill and maim people, the eyes of a man who could rape and murder and end up in maximum security.

She pulled away and moved back into the kitchen, and when she couldn't figure out what she wanted there, she went back to the living room, back to the door where she lingered for some time watching the night, and then she headed up-stairs which was damp with the steam and sweat and oils from his bath, and inside her room she bolted the door and shoved the antique dresser against it and sat down at the edge of the bed. Her face, she realized now, was wet and her hands were trembling. She sat on them and tried to calm her breathing. Her book on uncertainty stared up at her from the floor.

Fred, she moaned quietly into the night. Fred. She was afraid. Deathly afraid. But what could she do? She had to do something. She had to come up with a plan. She had to get out of there. Or get him the hell out. She saw that she was still shivering, that her hands were trembling, even her teeth were chattering. Her entire face was on fire. She grabbed a bottle from the bedside table and sprinkled some pills into her mouth. Then she stood up, blew out the candle, and crawled under the blanket, pulling and tucking it under her chin, and with her breath, she waited.

It rained steadily through the night and though it was at first impossible to sleep, she eventually drifted off, waking from time to time grateful for the snores wheezing through the house, which meant he had not killed her, he had not robbed her and left. At one point she got up to close a window down-stairs that had swung open in the wind, and when she saw him on the couch curled up like that, curled into a ball and shiver-ing and wheezing into the dark, she put another blanket on him. But as soon as she went to the door and paused in front of it, trying to decide how fast she could move, how far she could get, the wheezing stopped.

She woke to the smell of coffee and frying bacon. She woke to the warm sun pushing its way through the maple leaves outside and through her window and into her bed, falling in a square on her face. She woke to the life that she had impris-oned herself in. It wasn't Fred this time or her marriage. It was of her own doing.

She lit a cigarette. This was one of the things he hated, that she smoked; she drank to the point of drunkenness, she cursed, she loved sex, she read pulp, she liked violent movies, and she didn't always give a damn about his sermon when he was a preacher at a big evangelical church and had an image to uphold.

It was Thursday. On Thursdays she visited her mother who had Alzheimer's and lived in a nursing home three hours away. Usually she got there by noon, so they could have lunch. Her mother used to love oxtails and she had found a little Cuban place that braised them tenderly in tomato sauce and served them with small yellow-eyed pigeon peas mixed with saffron rice. Sometimes she'd read to her mother, recently they'd been working on a book about Sidney Poitier's life, and she'd sing show tunes and spirituals with her. Whatever she remembered. Her mother had taught piano and singing lessons for years. After that they would go for a walk in the botanical gardens nearby, then she would return her mother to her room and make the three-hour drive home. She looked forward to these outings with her mother dearly.

Downstairs on the counter he had scrambled eggs and the coffee was dripping steadily into the pot. She looked out the window at the wind-strewn grass that needed weeding; all the plants she had bought at Home Depot last week, intending to repot, were now blown to shreds or drowned. There was still no electricity and the room was quiet, no humming coming from the refrigerator or newscaster's voice buzzing from the television in the living room. Birds were busy at the feeder, noisy old jays and a few starlings. Is he even hygienic? she wondered, glancing at the plate of yellow eggs and then at his long and shapely fingers, the nails neatly cut and clean.

You might want to add salt, he said. I don't touch the stuff, high blood pressure.

He closed his eyes over his food, and then started to eat. The flashlight had left big angry welts on his face. This did not make her feel bad. He ate slowly, meditatively; he cut his bread into neat little squares with his knife, he chewed a long time as his dark bristled jaw, strong and square, moved up and down. He was wearing the pin-striped suit and the wrinkled shirt underneath was white and clean. He must've washed it last night. And the burgundy wingtips with his toes bunched up at the front were definitely not his size. He must've bludgeoned someone and taken his clothes and car. The felt hat sat proudly on the counter.

These are good eggs, he said to no one, must be organic. He looked at her and showed his teeth, which were big and bright and yellow. They don't have these where I'm coming from.

After they took Russell, her father had a break down, then a heart attack. After they took Russell, her father was no damn good.

She had no appetite whatsoever, and her food lay untouched, though after a while she played with the mushy eggs on her plate, using the fork to push them aside and then draw them toward her again. She had a CD she could cash and give to him. It had several more months still before maturity; they would charge her a penalty. Didn't matter, she would give it to him and then maybe he would go, he would drop off the face of the earth. That was her predicament: now that she had let him in, how to get him the hell out of her life.

Thank you for last night, he said softly, and she looked at him quickly, his eyes big and blue and full of light. She turned away. She wanted to tell him he must leave at once, but something was stopping her.

A minute later she went back upstairs and got dressed. Inside the bathroom mirror, her face was a mess, it had broken out, and a thousand boils had taken up residence. She got out her lotions, her rinses, and her special dermatology soaps, and after about half an hour she emerged with a new face and quarter-pound of foundation.

I'm going to the bank, she said to his back, the muscles moving slowly up and down under his jacket as he washed and dried the few plates. Her mug of coffee was sitting there untouched, her eggs too. He covered them up with a napkin.

I'm getting you some money so you can go, she said, so you can start again.

He turned then to look at her, his eyes hard and still. There was a warning in them and his whole face had turned to stone. She saw how he could kill. Easily.

I'm not going to the police, she said, I'm going to the bank. Suddenly she felt testy. If this were about the police, I would've handed you over last night. Don't you want to have a life? Don't you want freedom? She saw something shift in his face and it emboldened her. You have to trust me too. This works both ways. I had to trust you last night and that wasn't easy.

Outside, the air was incredibly humid and the men working for the cable and electric companies were already attached to posts repairing wires; police cars rolled slowly up and down the street as if looking for somebody, and the dog walkers were out too, with their baggies of brown stool. Young mothers pushed their expensive strollers and joggers, delighted to see the sun again, daintily sidestepped puddles of water. Hard to believe that not too long ago this was considered an old working-class neighborhood full of mainly Irish and Italians who worked in the arsenal. Now the town was full of yuppies driving up property taxes and opening restaurants that served arugula salads and Kobe organic burgers. And the arsenal now housed the gourmet ghetto, expensive artist studios, condominiums, and a high-priced mall.

She walked by the tiny cemetery where many a dog went to defecate against the mildewed tombstones, and by the old church they were developing into more condominiums. She waited at the light, and when it changed she walked past the hairdressing salon, the Syrian shoe repair shop, the Greek diner, and the Miles Pratt house, taken over by dentists now. She nodded hello to a man and his little girl standing outside the Armenian Library and Museum. Down the tiny side street near the CVS was the Iranian restaurant where she'd had lunch a few times by herself; she liked the rice sprinkled with fleshy pomegranate, the ice cream flavored with cardamom and rose water, and had planned to take her daughters there when they visited. To the left of the restaurant was the post office, and beyond that the Charles River, with its cool, dark, slow-moving waters. Often she went there to read or to feed the ducks even though there was a big sign prohibiting this. Sometimes just to empty her head and to be in the company of nature.

Outside the bank, she sat on the bench near a Japanese maple and smoked three cigarettes in succession, waiting for the line to thin. Up the street near the CVS, a police car circled the square slowly.

PART II

SKELETONS IN THE CLOSET

FEMME SOLE

BY DANA CAMERON

North End

A moment of your time, Anna Hoyt."

Anna slowed and cursed to herself. She'd seen Adam Seaver as she crossed Prince Street, and for a terrible moment thought he was following her. She'd hoped to lose him amid the peddlers and shoppers at the busy market near Dock Square, but she couldn't ignore him after he called out. His brogue was no more than a low growl, but conversations around him tended to fade and die. He never raised his voice, but he never had a problem making himself heard, even over the loudest of Boston's boisterous hawkers.

In fact, with anxious glances, the crowd melted back in retreat from around her. No one wanted to be between Seaver and whatever he was after.

Cowards, she thought. But her own mouth was dry as he approached.

She turned, swallowed, met his eyes, then lowered hers, hoping it looked like modesty or respect and not revulsion. His face was weathered and, in places, blurred with scars, marks of fights from which he'd walked away the winner; there was a nick above his ear where he'd had his head shaved. Seaver smiled; she could see two rows of sharp, ugly teeth like a mouthful of broken glass or like one of the bluefish the men sometimes caught in the harbor. Bluefish were so vicious they had to be clubbed when they were brought into the boat or they'd shear your finger off.

He didn't touch her, but she flinched when he gestured to a quiet space behind the stalls. It was blustery autumn, salt air and a hint of snow to come, but a sour milk smell nearly gagged her. Dried leaves skittered over discarded rotten vegetables, or was it that even the boldest rats fled when Seaver approached?

"How are you, Mr. Seaver ?" she asked. She tried to imagine that she was safely behind her bar. She felt she could manage anything with the bar between her and the rest of the world.

"Fair enough. Yourself?"

"Fine." She wished he'd get on with it. "Thanks." His excessive manners worried her. He'd never spoken to her before, other than to order his rum and thank her.

When he didn't speak, Anna felt the sweat prickle along the hairline at the back of her neck. The wind blew a little colder, and the crowd and imagined safety of the market seemed remote. The upright brick structure of the Town House was impossibly far away, and the ships anchored groaning at the wharves could have been at sea.

He waited, searched her face, then looked down. "What very pretty shoes."

"Thank you. They're from Turner's." She shifted uncomfortably. She didn't believe he was interested in her shoes, but neither did she imagine he was trying to spare her feelings by not staring at the bruises that ran up the side of her head. These were almost hidden with an artfully draped shawl, but her lip was still visibly puffy. It was too easy to trace the line from that to the black and blue marks. One mark led to the next like a constellation.

One thing always led to another.

"What can I do for you, Mr. Seaver?" she said at last. Not knowing was too much.

"I may be in a way to do something for you."

Anna couldn't help it: she sighed. She heard the offer five times a night.

"Nothing like that," he said, showing that rank of teeth. "It's your husband."

"What about him?" Gambling debts, whores, petty theft? Another harebrained investment gone west? Her mind raced over the many ways Thomas could have offended Mr. Seaver.

"I saw him at Clark's law office this morning. I had business with Clark . . . on behalf of my employer . . ."

Anna barely stifled a shudder. Best to know nothing of Seaver or his employer's business, which had brought a fortune so quickly that it could only have come from some brutal trade in West Indian contraband. Thick Thomas Hoyt was well beneath the notice of Seaver's boss, praise God.

". . . and your husband was still talking to Clark."

"Yes?" Anna refused to reveal surprise at Thomas visiting a lawyer. He had no use or regard for the law.

"He was asking how he could sell your establishment."

"He can't. It's mine," she said before thinking.

Seaver showed no surprise at her vehemence. "Much as I thought, and exactly what Clark told him. Apparently, Hook Miller wants the place."

"So he said last night. I thanked him, but I'm not selling. He was more than understanding."

Seaver tilted his head. "Because he thinks the way to acquire your tavern is through your husband."

The words went through Anna like a knife, and she understood. Her hand rose to her cheek. The beating had come only hours after Miller's offer and her refusal. Thomas had been blind drunk, and she could barely make out what had driven him this time.

"If I sell it, how will we live? The man's an idiot." She was shocked to realize that she'd actually said this, that she was having a conversation, *this* conversation, with Seaver.

"Perhaps Thomas thinks he can weasel a big enough price from Miller."

"The place is *mine*. No one can take it, not even my husband. My father said so. He showed me the papers." *Feme sole merchant* were what the lawyers called her, with their fancy Latin. The documents allowed her to conduct business almost as if she was a man. At first, it was only with her father's consent, but as she prospered—and he sickened—it was accepted that she was responsible, allowed to trade on her own. Very nearly independent, almost as good as a man, in the year of Our Lord 1745. And, though she could never say so aloud, better than most.

"I think Clark will be bound by the document," Seaver said. "At least until someone more persuasive than Thomas comes along."

The list of people more persuasive and smarter than her husband was lengthy.

"It's only a piece of paper." Seaver shrugged. "A fragile thing."

Anna nodded, trying not to shift from one foot to another. Eventually, Hook Miller would find a way. As long as she'd known him, he always had.

Anna swallowed. "Why are you telling me this?"

He shrugged. "I like to drink at your place."

She almost believed him. "And?"

She knew what was coming, was nearly willing to pay the price that Seaver would ask. Whatever would save her property and livelihood, the modicum of security and independence she'd struggled to achieve. What were her alternatives? Sew until she was blind, or follow behind some rich bitch and carry *her* purse, run *her* errands? Turn a sailor's whore?

"And?" she repeated.

"And." He leered. "I want to see what you will do."

The bad times were hard for everyone, but it was the good times that brought real trouble, she thought. A pretty young lass with no family and a thriving business on the waterfront. She might as well have hung out a sign.

Anna hurried back to the Queen's Arms, shopping forgotten. No one had ever paid the property any attention when her father ran the place. It was only after she'd taken over the tavern, within sight of the wharves that cut into Boston Harbor, that business grew and drew attention.

The Queen was a neighborhood place on Fleet Street. "The burying ground up behind you, and the deep, dark sea ahead," her father used to say, but in between was a place for a man to drink his beer after work—or before, as may be the case—the occasional whiskey, if he was feeling full and fat. Or three or five, if he was broke and buggered.

She stumbled over the cobbles in the street, but recovered and hurried along, needing to reassure herself the place was still there, that it hadn't vanished, hadn't been whisked away by magic from the crowd of buildings that lined the narrow streets above the harbor. Or been burned to the ground, more likely. She never doubted that her husband, stupid as he was, would find a way to rob her for Miller, if that's what Thomas imagined he wanted.

Had Thomas Hoyt been content with hot meals twice a day, too much to drink and ten minutes sweating over his wife on Saturday night, church and repentance Sunday morning, Anna could have managed him well enough. She wanted a more ambitious man, but Thomas had come with his mother's shop next door. When that allowed Anna to expand her tavern, she thought it a fair enough trade.

Until she discovered Thomas *was* ambitious, in his own way. While she poured ale, rum, and whiskey, he sat in the corner. Ready to change the barrels or quell the occasional rowdiness, he more often read his paper and smoked, playing the host. His eyes followed his pretty wife's movements and those of all the men around her.

There were two men he had watched with peculiar interest, and Anna now understood why. One was Hook, named Robert Miller by his mother, a ruffian with a finger in every pie and a hand in every pocket. Hook's gang were first to take advantage of all the trade on the waterfront, from loading and unloading ships to smuggling. But he did more for the local men than he took from them and was a kind of hero for it. Of course Hook appealed to Thomas: he was everything Thomas imagined he himself could be.

The other man he watched was Seaver, but even Thomas was smart enough to be circumspect when he did it. When one of Miller's men drunkenly pulled Seaver from his chair one night, claiming his looks were souring the beer, Seaver left without a word. But he came back the next night, and Miller's man never did. That man now drank at another house, where no one knew him. Three fingers from his right hand were broken and his nose bitten off.

The other men left Seaver alone after that. Anna smiled as she served his rum, but it stopped at her eyes. He was content to sit quietly, alone with who knew what thoughts.

Thomas was scrubbing the bar when she arrived. He looked up, smiled as though he remembered nothing of what had happened the night before. Maybe he didn't.

"There's my girl. Shopping done?"

"I forgot something."

"Well, find it and I'll walk you to the dressmaker's myself. It's getting dark."

He said it as though the dark brought devils instead of the tradesmen who came regularly to her place. Who worshipped her. She had married him a year before, after her father died, for protection. She ran her tongue along the inside of her cheek, felt the swelling there, felt a tooth wiggle, her lip tear a fraction.

"I won't have you be less than the best-dressed lady in the North End," he said expansively, as if he emptied his pockets onto the counter himself. Anna and Mr. Long, the tailor, had a deal: Anna borrowed the latest gowns; wearing them, she showed them to perfection, the ideal advertisement with her golden hair and slim waist. The men at her place either sent their wives to the dressmaker's so they'd look more like Anna, or spent more money at Anna's just to look at her, a fine, soft, pretty thing amid so much coarseness.

She pretended to locate some trifle under the bar, and Thomas wiped his hands on the seat of his britches. She forced a smile; her mouth still hurt. Better to have him think she was stupid or in love. Even better, afraid.

"The best news, Anna," he said, taking her arm as they went back onto the street. "Rob Miller has added another twenty pounds to his asking price. We were right to wait."

It was still less than half the value of the place. Under no circumstances would she consider selling to Hook Miller and give Thomas the money to invest and lose.

She nodded, as if her refusal to sell had been a joint decision.

"I think we'll wait until Friday, see if we can't drive the price a little higher," he said, patting her hand. His palm was heavy and rough. She saw the faint abrasions along the knuckles, remembered them intimately.

She nodded again, kept her eyes on her feet, shoes peeping out from under her skirt, as she moved briskly to keep up with Thomas. He raced across the cobbles, she a half-pace behind.

Friday, then. Three days. Between Miller's desire for her tavern and Thomas's wish to impress him, she was trapped.

Friday night came despite Anna's prayers for fire, a hurricane, a French invasion. But the place was as it always was: a wide, long room, stools and tables, two good chairs by a large, welcoming fire. The old windows were in good repair, the leads tight, and decent curtains kept out the drafts. The warm smells of good Barbadian rum and local ale kept the world at bay.

When Miller came into the tavern, Thomas got up immediately, offered him the best upholstered seat, nearest the fire. Miller dismissed him outright, said his business was with Anna. Anna tried with all her might to divert his attention back to Thomas, but Miller could not have made more of a show of favoring her in front of the entire room, who watched from behind raised mugs. Thomas glowered, his gaze never leaving Anna.

"Why won't you sell the place, Anna?" Miller's words and tone were filled with hurt; she was doing him unfairly.

Anna's eyes flicked around the room; the men sitting

there drinking were curious. Why would Anna cross Miller? No profit in that, they all knew.

"And if I did, what would I live on then?" she asked gaily, as if Miller had been revisiting a long-standing joke.

"Go to the country, for all of me," he said, draining his glass. It might as well have been *Go to the Devil.*

As if she had a farm to retire to, a home somewhere other than over the barroom. "I promised my father I would not," she said, trying to maintain the tone of a joke, but the strain was audible in her voice, her desperation a tremor in her answer.

"Well, come find me—" he set his empty glass down. "When you're ready to be reasonable." He tipped his hat to her, ignored Thomas, and left.

After that, the other regulars filed out, one by one. None wanted to see what they all knew would come next. Anna tried to entice them to stay, even offering a round on the house on the flimsy excuse of someone's good haul of fish. But it couldn't last forever, and eventually even the boy who helped serve was sent home. Only Seaver was left.

It was late, past the time when Thomas generally retired. It was obvious he wasn't going to bed.

Seaver stood up. Anna looked at him with a wild hope. Perhaps he would come to her aid, somehow defuse the situation. He put a coin down on the counter and leaned toward her.

She glanced hastily at Thomas, who was scowling as he jabbed the fire with a poker. Anna's face was a mask of desperation. She leaned closer, and Seaver surreptitiously ran a finger along the back of her hand.

"Better if you don't argue with him," he breathed, his lips barely moving. "Don't fight back too much."

She watched his back as he left. The room was empty, quiet, save for the crackle of the fire, the beating of Anna's heart in her chest.

Thomas straightened, and turned. "I thought we had an agreement."

Anna looked around; there was no one to help her. The door . . .

"I thought, any man comes in here looking for a piece, you send him up to that fancy cathouse on Salem Street. And yet I see you, a damned slut, making cow eyes at every man in here, right in front of me."

She ran, but just as her fingers touched the latch, she felt the poker slam across her shoulders. She cried out, fell against the door. The next blows landed on her back, but Thomas, tired of imprecision and mindful of leaving visible marks that would make the punters uneasy, dropped the poker and relied on the toe of his boot.

When his rage diminished, Thomas stormed out. Anna remained on the floor, too afraid and too hurt to get up. She measured the grain of the wood planks while she thought. Thomas would go to Miller, reassure him the sale was imminent. Soon she would have no choice.

She eventually forced herself up, pulling herself onto a stool. No bones broken, this time.

In her quest to find security, independence, she'd first tried the law, and when that wasn't enough, she'd put her faith in her husband's strength. Now . . . she wasn't sure what would work, but knew she would be damned if she gave in. Not after all she'd done to make the place her own. Her father had taught her the value of a business, repeated it over and over, as she held his hand while he died. He said there were only two books she needed to mind, her Bible and her ledger, but now the latter had her in deep trouble. She moved stiffly to the bar, poured herself a large rum, drank it down neat, exchanging the burn of the liquor for the searing pain in her back.

Thomas didn't return in the morning, but Anna hadn't expected him to. He often stayed away after a beating, a chance for her to think over her sins, he'd told her once before. But never for more than a day or two.

She moved stiffly that day, easier the next, but late the third evening, when Anna was about to bar the door for the night, a man's hand shoved it open. Maybe Thomas had had a change of heart, had come home—

It was Hook Miller.

She didn't offer a drink. He didn't ask for one.

"Why not sell to me, Anna Hoyt?" he asked, warming his hands at the fire. "I want this place, so you might as well save yourself the trouble."

"I told you: my father said I should never sell. Property—it's the only sure thing in this world."

Miller didn't seem bothered, only a bit impatient. "There's nothing sure, Anna. Wood burns, casks break, and customers leave. And I've had the lawyer Clark make your rights over to Thomas. Take my money, leave here."

She said nothing. Felt the paper she kept in her shoe, the copy of the document that gave her the Queen's Arms, the property, the right to do business. Now they were, he was telling her, worthless. After all her work, all she'd done . . .

Suddenly, Anna had a dreadful thought. "Where's Thomas? Have you seen him?"

"Indeed, I have just left him." Miller stood straight, smiled crookedly. He continued, mock-serious: "He's . . . down by my wharf. He couldn't persuade you to sell, but he's still looking after your interests."

The blood froze inside her. Thomas was dead, she knew it.

Miller tilted his head and waited. When she couldn't bring herself to respond, he left, closing the door behind him.

The paralyzing cold spread over her, and, for a blessed moment, Anna felt nothing. Then the shivering started, brought her back to the tavern. Anna's first thought was that her knees would give way before she reached the chair by the fire. She clutched the back of it, her nails digging into the upholstery. When she felt one of them snap, she turned, took three steps, then vomited into the slops pot on the bar.

Better, Anna thought, wiping her mouth. I must be better than this.

Still trembling, but at least able to think, she climbed the stairs to her rooms. She saw Thomas's good shirt hanging from a peg, and buried her face in it, breathing deeply. She took it down, rubbing the thick linen between her fingers, and considered the length of the sleeves. She stared at the peg, high on the wall, and reluctantly made her decision.

Everything was different in her new shoes. Since she was used to her thin slippers, the cobbles felt oddly distant beneath the thick soles, and it took her awhile to master the clunkiness of the heels. She relied on a population used to drunken sailors to ignore her, relied on the long cloak to conceal most of her blunders. Thomas's clothes would have been impossible, but she still had a chest full of her father's things, and his boots were a better fit. Best not to think about the rest of her garb. She needed to confirm what Miller had hinted, and she couldn't be seen doing it. Anna was too familiar a figure to those whose lives were spent on the wharves, and most of them would be friendly faces. But not if she were caught. If they caught her, so scandalously dressed in britches, well . . . losing the tavern would be the least of it.

Somehow, her need to know for sure was stronger than fear, than embarrassment, and the bell in the Old North Church chimed as she found her way to Miller's wharf. The reek of tar and wood fires made her eyes water, and a stiff breeze combined drying fish with the smells of spices in nearby warehouses, making her almost gag.

The moon broke through the clouds. She walked out to the harbor, feeling more and more exposed by the moment . . .

Nothing on Miller's wharf that shouldn't be there. She stopped, struck by a realization. Hook would never lay the murder at his own doorstep.

The urge to move a short way down to the pier and wharf that belonged to Clark, Miller's detested rival in business, was nearly physical.

At first, Anna saw nothing but the boards of the pier itself. She climbed down the ladder to the water's edge, hooked one of the dinghies by its rope, and pulled it close. She boarded, cast off, and rowed, following the length of the pier. Though she preferred to be secret, there was no need to muffle the oarlocks; the waterfront's activity died down at night, but it was never completely silent along the water. Sweat trickled down her back even as thin ice crackled on the floor of the boat beneath her feet.

The half hour rang out, echoed by church bells across Boston and Charlestown, and Anna shivered in spite of her warm exercise.

Three-quarters of the way down the pier, Anna saw a glimpse of white on the water. She uncovered her lantern and held it up.

Among the pilings, beneath the pier, all manner of lost and discarded things floated, bobbing idly on top of the waves: broken crate wood, a dead seagull, an unmoored float. There was something else.

A body.

Even without seeing his face, she knew it was Thomas, his fair hair floating like kelp, the shirt she herself had patched billowing around him like sea foam. A wave broke against the piling of the pier and one of his hands was thrust momentarily to the surface, puffy and raw: the fish and harbor creatures had already been to feast.

Anna stared awhile, and then maneuvered the boat around. She rowed quietly back to the ladder, tied up the dinghy, and headed home.

She brought the bottle of rum to her room, drank until the cold was chased away and she could feel her fingers again. Then she drank a good deal more. She changed back into her own clothing and, keeping her father's advice in mind, opened her Bible. In an old habit, she let it fall open where it would, closing her eyes and placing a finger on the text. The candle burned low while she read, waiting for someone to come and tell her Thomas Hoyt was dead.

Hook Miller came to the burial on Copp's Hill. As he made his way up to where Anna stood, the crowd of neighbors—there were nearly fifty of them, for nothing beat a good funeral—doffed their hats out of respect to his standing. Miller's clothes were showy but ill-suited to him, Anna knew, and he pretended concern that was as foreign to him as a clean handkerchief. He even waited decently before he approached her, and those nearby heard a generous offer of aid to the widow, so that she could retreat to a quieter life elsewhere.

The offering price was still an affront. When she shook her head, he nodded sadly, said he'd be back when she was more composed. She knew it wasn't solicitousness but the eyes of the neighborhood that made him so nice. The next time Miller approached her, it would be in private. There would be no refusing that offer.

When Seaver came in for his drink later, she avoided his glance. She'd already made up her mind.

The next morning, she sent a note to Hook Miller. No reason to be seen going to him, when there was nothing more natural than for him to come to the tavern. And if his visit stood out among others, why, she was a propertied widow now, who had to keep an eye to the future.

He didn't bother knocking, came in as if he already owned the place, and barred the door behind him. She was standing behind a chair, waiting, a bottle of wine on the table, squat-bodied and long-necked, along with two of her best glasses, polished to gleaming. One was half-filled, half-drunk. The fire was low, and there were only two candles lit.

He bowed and sat without being asked. His breath was thick with harsh New England rum. "Well?"

"I can't sell the place. I'd be left with nothing."

Miller was silent at first, but his eyes narrowed. "And?"

Anna straightened. "Marry me. That way . . . the place will be yours, and I'll be . . . looked after."

"You didn't sign it over to Thomas."

"Thomas Hoyt was as thick as two short planks. I couldn't trust him to find his arse with both hands."

Thomas's absence now was not discussed.

Miller pondered. "If I do, you'll sign the Queen's Arms over to me."

"The day we wed." Her father had given her the hope and the means, but then slowly, painfully, she'd discovered she couldn't keep the place alone. She swallowed. "I can't do this by myself."

"And what benefit to me to marry you?"

Her hours of thought had prepared the answer. "You'll get a property you've always wanted, and with it, an eye and an ear to everything that happens all along the waterfront. More than that: respectability. This whole neighborhood is getting nothing but richer, and you'd be in the middle of it. What better way to advance than through deals with the merchant nobs themselves? To say nothing of window dressing for your other . . . affairs."

Miller laughed, then stopped, considered what she was saying. "Sharp. And a clever wife to entertain my new friends? It makes sense."

"Those merchants, they're no more than a step above hustling themselves. We can be of use to each other," she said carefully. She'd almost said *need*, but that would have been fatal. "Wine?"

He looked at her, looked at the bottle, the one empty glass. "Thanks."

She poured, the ruby liquid turning blood-black in the green-tinged glasses, against the dark of the room.

He stared at the glass, his brow furrowing. "I've more of a mind for beer, if you don't mind."

She looked disappointed, but didn't press him. "You'll have to get a head for wine if you expect to move up in the world." She rose and slid a pewter mug from a peg on the wall, then filled it from the large barrel behind her bar.

Miller smiled, thanked her. She raised her glass to him, sipped. He saluted and drank too.

It was then he noticed the large Bible on the table next to them. He reached over, flipped through carelessly.

"Too much theater for one about to be so soon remarried, don't you think?" He flicked through the pages, as if looking for something he could make use of. "Devotion doesn't play. Not around here, anyway."

Anna suppressed her feelings at seeing him handle the book so roughly. She shut it firmly, moved it away. "My father said it was the only book besides my ledger to heed."

Miller shrugged. Piety was unexpected, especially after her reaction—or lack thereof—to her husband's murder, but who could pretend to understand a woman? Her reaction aroused him, however. Any resistance did. "Let me see what I'll be getting myself into. Lift your skirts."

Anna had known it would come to this; still, she hesitated. Only a moment. But before Hook had to say another word, she bunched up the silk, slippery in her sweaty palms, and raised her skirts to her thighs. Miller reached out, grabbed the ribbon of her garter, and pulled. It slithered out of its knot, draped itself over his fist. He leaned forward, slid a finger over the top of her stocking, then collapsed onto the table. His head hit hard, and he didn't say another word.

Repulsed, Anna unhooked his finger from her stocking, let his hand fall heavily, smack against the chair leg. She straightened her stocking, retied her garter, then picked up the heavy Bible. She hesitated, gulping air, then, remembering her father's words and the fourth chapter of Judges, nodded.

I must be better than this. I must manage.

She reached into the cracked binding of the Bible and withdrew a long steel needle. Its point picked up the light from the candle and glittered. Her breath held, she stood over the unconscious man, then, aiming carefully, she drove it deep into his ear.

Shortly, with a grunt, a shudder, a sigh, Miller stopped breathing.

She had been afraid she'd been too stingy, miscalculated the dose, unseen in the bottom of the pewter mug, not wanting to warn him with the smell of belladonna or have it spill as it waited on the peg. Her father had been frailer, older, and when she could stand his rasping, rattling breathing no longer, could wait no longer to begin her own plans for the Queen's Arms, she had mixed a smaller amount into his beer. No matter: either the poison or the needle had done its work on Hook Miller.

Anna threw the rest of the beer onto the floor, followed it with the last of the wine from the bottle. No sense in taking chances. She had a long night ahead of her. She could barely move Hook on her own. Slender though she was, she was strong from hauling water and kegs and wood from the time she could walk, but he was nearly two hundred pounds of dead meat. She'd planned this, though, with as much meticulousness as she planned everything in her life. Everything that could be anticipated, that is. Thomas's ill-conceived greediness she hadn't counted on, nor Miller's interest in her place. These were hard lessons and dearly bought.

She would be better. She would manage.

She went to the back, brought out the barrow used to move stock. With careful work, and a little luck, Anna tipped Miller from his chair into the barrow, and, struggling to keep her balance, wheeled him out of the public room into the back kitchen ell. She left him there, out of sight, and checked again that the back door was still barred. She twitched the curtain so that it hung completely over the small window.

Lighting a taper from the fireplace, she considered her plan. A change of clothes, from silk into something for scut work. She had hours of dirty business ahead of her, as bad and dirty as slaughtering season, but really, it was no different from butchering a hog.

A small price to pay for her freedom and the time to plan how better to keep it.

Holding the taper, she hurried up the narrow back stairs to the chamber over the public room. When she opened the door, her breath caught in her throat. There was a lit candle on the table across from her bed.

Adam Seaver was sitting in her best chair.

Anna felt her mouth parch. Although she'd half expected to be interrupted in her work, she hadn't thought it would be in her own chamber. But Seaver had wanted to see what she'd do—he'd said so himself. She swallowed two or three times before she could ask.

"How?"

"You should nail up that kitchen window. It's too easy to reach in and shove the bar from the door. Then up the stairs, just as you yourself came. But not before I watched you with Miller." He pulled an unopened bottle from his pocket, cut the red wax from the stopper, opened it. "I'll pour my own drinks, thanks. What is the verse? *After she gave him drink, Jael went unto him with a peg of the tent and smote the nail into his temple?*"

"Near enough."

"A mistake teaching women to read. But then, if you couldn't read, you couldn't figure your books, and you wouldn't have such a brisk business as you do." He drank. "A double-edged sword. But as nice a bit of needlework as I've ever seen from a lady."

Keep breathing, Anna. You're not done yet. "What now?" She thought of the pistol in the trunk by the bed, the knife under her pillow. They might as well have been at the bottom of the harbor.

"A bargain. You're a widow with a tavern, I'm the agent of an important man. You also have a prime piece of real estate, and an eye on everything that happens along here. And, it seems, an eye to advancement. I think we can deal amiably enough, and to our mutual benefit."

At that moment, Anna almost wished Seaver would just cut her throat. She'd never be free of this succession of men, never able to manage by herself. The rage welled up in her, as it had never done before, and she thought she would choke on it. Then she remembered the paper hidden in her shoe, the document that made the tavern and its business wholly her own, and how she'd fought for it. She'd be damned before she handed it over to another man.

But she saw Seaver watching her carefully and it came to her. Perhaps like Miller not immediately grasping that the obvious next move for him was civil life and nearly legitimate trade— with all its fat skimming—she was not ambitious enough. Instead of mere survival, relying on the tavern, she could parlay it into more. Working with Seaver, who, after all, was only the errand boy of one of the most powerful—and dangerous—men in New England, she might do more than survive. She saw the beginning of a much wider, much richer future.

The whole world open to her, if she kept sharp. If she could be better than she was.

She went over to the mantel, took down a new bottle, opened it, poured herself a drink. Raised the glass.

She would pour her own drinks, and Seaver would pour his own.

She would manage.

"To our mutual benefit," she toasted.

THE DARK ISLAND

BY BRENDAN DuBOIS

Boston Harbor

S he was waiting for me when I came back from the corner store and I stopped, giving her a quick scan. She had on a dark blue dress, black sensible shoes, and a small blue hat balanced on the back of thick brown hair. She held a small black leather purse in her hands, like she knew she was in a dangerous place and was frightened to lose it. On that last part, she was right, for it was evening and she was standing in Scollay Square, with its lights, horns, music, honky-tonks, burlesque houses, and hordes of people with sharp tastes who came here looking for trouble, and more often than not, found it.

I brushed past a group of drunk sailors in their dress blues as I got up to my corner, the sailors no doubt happy that with the war over, they didn't have to worry about crazed kamikazes smashing into their gun turrets, burning to death out there in the Pacific. They were obviously headed to one of the nearby bars. There were other guys out there as well, though I could always identify the ones who were recently discharged vets: they moved quickly, their eyes flicking around, and whenever there was a loud horn or a backfire from a passing truck, they would freeze in place.

And then, of course, they would unfreeze. There were years of drinking and raising hell to catch up on.

I shifted my paper grocery sack from one hand to the other

and approached the woman, touched the brim of my fedora with my free hand. "Are you waiting for me?" I asked.

Her face was pale and frightened, like a young mom seeing blood on her child for the very first time. "Are you Billy Sullivan?"

"Yep."

"Yes, I'm here to see you."

I shrugged. "Then follow me, miss."

I moved past her and opened the wooden door that led to a small foyer, and then upstairs, the wooden steps creaking under our footfalls. At the top, a narrow hallway led off, three doors on each side, each door with a half-frame of frosted glass. Mine said, *B. Sullivan, Investigations*, and two of the windows down the hallway were blank. The other three announced a watchmaker, a piano teacher, and a press agent.

I unlocked the door, flicked on the light, and walked in. There was an old oak desk in the center with my chair, a Remington typewriter on a stand, and two solid filing cabinets with locks. In front of the desk were two wooden chairs, and I motioned my guest to the nearest one. A single window that hadn't been washed since Hoover was president overlooked the square and its flickering neon lights.

"Be right back," I said, ducking through a curtain off to the side. Beyond the curtain was a small room with a bed, radio, easy chair, table lamp, and icebox. A closed door led to a small bathroom that most days had plenty of hot water. I put a bottle of milk away, tossed the bread on a counter next to the toaster and hot plate, and returned to the office. I took off my coat and hat, and hung both on a coat rack.

The woman sat there, leaning forward a bit, like she didn't want her back to be spoiled by whatever cooties resided in my office. She looked at me and tried to smile. "I thought all private detectives carried guns."

I shook my head. "Like the movies? Roscoes, heaters, gats, all that nonsense? Nah, I saw enough guns the last couple of years. I don't need one, not for what I do."

At my desk, I uncapped my Parker pen and grabbed a legal pad. "You know my name, don't you think you should return the favor?"

She nodded quickly. "Of course. The name is Mandy Williams . . . I'm from Seattle."

I looked up. "You're a long way from home."

Tears formed in the corners of her eyes. "I know, I know . . . and it's all going to sound silly, but I hope you can help me find something."

"Something or some*one*?" I asked.

"Something," she said. "Something that means the world to me."

"Go on."

"This is going to sound crazy, Mister Sullivan, so please . . . bear with me, all right?"

"Sure."

She took a deep breath. "My fiancé, Roger Thompson, he was in the army and was stationed here, before he was shipped overseas."

I made a few notes on the pad, kept my eye on her.

"We kept in touch, almost every day, writing letters back and forth, sending each other mementos. Photos, souvenirs, stuff like that . . . and he told me he kept everything I sent to him in a shoe box in his barracks. And I told him I did the same . . . kept everything that he sent to me."

Now she opened her purse, took out a white tissue, which she dabbed at her eyes. "Silly, isn't it . . . it's been nearly a year

. . . I know I'm not making sense, it's just that Roger didn't come back. He was killed a few months before the war was over."

My hand tightened on the pen. "Sorry to hear that."

"Oh, what can you do, you know? And ever since then, well, I've gone on, you know? Have even thought about dating again . . . and then . . ."

The tissue went back to work and I waited. So much of my professional life is waiting, waiting for a phone call, waiting for someone to show up, waiting for a bill to be paid.

She coughed and continued: "Then, last month, I got a letter from a buddy of his. Name of Greg Fleming. Said they were bunkmates here. And they shipped out together, first to France and then to the frontlines. And Greg told me that Roger said that before he left, he hid that shoe box in his barracks. He was afraid the box would get lost or spoiled if he brought it overseas with him."

"I see," I said, though I was practically lying. "And why do you need me? Why not go to the base and sweet talk the duty officer, and find the barracks your fiancé was staying at?"

"Because . . . because the place he was training at, it's been closed since the war was over. And it's not easy to get to."

"Where is it?"

Another dab of the tissue. "It's out on Boston Harbor. On one of the islands. Gallops Island. That's where Roger was stationed."

The place was familiar to me. "Yeah, I remember Gallops. It was used as a training facility. For cooks, radiomen, and medics. What did your man train for?"

"Radioman," she said simply. "Later . . . later I found out that being a radioman was so very dangerous. You were out in the open, and German snipers liked to shoot at a radioman and the officer standing next to him . . . that's, that's what happened to Roger. There was some very fierce fighting and he was . . . he was . . . oh God, they blew his head off . . ."

And then she bowed and started weeping in her tissue, and I sat there, feeling like my limbs were made of cement, for I didn't know what the hell to do. Finally I cleared my throat and said, "Sorry, miss . . . Look, can I get you something to drink?"

The tissue was up against her face and she shook her head. "No, no, I don't drink."

I pushed away from my desk. "I was thinking of something a bit less potent. I'll be right back."

About ten minutes later, I came back with two chipped white china mugs and passed one over to her. She took a sip and seemed surprised. "Tea?"

"Yeah," I said, sitting back down. "A bit of a secret, so please don't tell on me, okay? You know the reputation we guys like to maintain."

She smiled, and I felt I had won a tiny victory. "How in the world did you ever start drinking tea?"

I shrugged. "Picked up the habit when I was stationed in England."

"You were in the army?"

I nodded. "Yep."

"What did you do?"

I took a sip from my own mug. "Military police. Spent a lot of time guarding fences and ammo dumps or directing traffic. Pretty boring. Never really heard a shot fired in anger, though a couple of times I did hear Kraut artillery as we were heading east when I got over to France."

"So you know war, then."

"I do."

"And I'm sure you know loss as well."

Again, the tightening of my hand. "Yeah, I know loss."

And she must have sensed a change in my voice, for she stared harder at me and said, "Who was he?"

I couldn't speak for a moment, and then I said, "My older brother. Paul."

"What happened?"

I suppose I should have kept my mouth shut, but there was something about her teary eyes that just got to me. I cleared my throat. "He was 82nd Airborne. Wounded at the Battle of the Bulge. Mortar shrapnel. They were surrounded by the Krauts, and I guess it took a long time for him to die . . ."

"Then we both know, don't we."

"Yeah." I looked down at the pad of paper. "So. What do you need me for?"

She twisted the crumpled bit of tissue in her hands. "I . . . I don't know how to get to that island. I've sent letters to everyone I can think of, in the army and in Congress, and no one can help me out . . . and I found out that the island is now restricted. There's some sort of new radar installation being built there . . . no one can land on the island."

I knew where this was going but I wanted to hear it from her. "All right, but let me say again, Miss Williams, why do you need me?"

She waited, waited for what seemed to be a long time. She took a long sip from her tea. There were horns from outside, a siren, and I could hear music from the nearest burlesque hall. "Um . . . well, I've been here for a week . . . asking around . . . at the local police station . . . asking about a detective who might help me, one from around here, one who knows the harbor islands . . ."

"And my name came up? Really? From who?"

"A . . . a desk sergeant. Name of O'Connor."

I grimaced. Fat bastard, never got over the fact that my dad beat up his dad ten or fifteen years ago at some Irish tavern in Southie; he always gave me crap, every time he saw me. "All right. What did he tell you?"

"That you used to work with your dad in the harbor, pulling in lobster pots, working after school and summers, and he said . . . well, he said . . ."

"Go on, Miss Williams. What did he say?"

"He said that if anyone could get me out to the islands and back, it'd be that thick-skulled mick Billy Sullivan."

I tried not to smile. "Yeah, that sounds like the good sergeant."

Her voice softened. "Please, Mister Sullivan. I . . . I don't know what else to do. I can't make it out there without your help, and getting those memories from my man . . . that would mean the world to me."

"If the island is off-limits during the day, it means we'll have to go out at night. Do you understand, Miss Williams?"

She seemed a bit surprised. "I . . . I thought I could draw you a map, a description, something like that."

I shook my head. "Not going to work. I'm not going out to Gallops Island at night without you. If I find that box of mementos for you, I want you right there, to check it out."

"But—"

"If that's going to be a problem, Miss Williams, then I'm afraid I can't help you."

My potential client sounded meek. "I . . . I don't like boats . . . but no, it won't be a problem."

"Good. My rate is fifty dollars a day, plus expenses . . . but this should be relatively easy. And that fifty dollars has to be paid in advance."

She opened her purse, deftly pulled out three tens and a twenty, which I scooped up and put into my top desk drawer. I tore off a sheet of paper, wrote something down, and slid it over to her. "There. Address in South Boston. Little fishing and tackle shop, with a dock to the harbor. I'll see you there tomorrow at 6 p.m. Weather permitting, it should be easy."

My new client folded up the piece of paper and put it in her purse, and then stood up, held out a hand with manicured red nails. "Oh, I can't thank you enough, Mister Sullivan. This means so much to me, and . . ."

I shook her hand and said, "It's too early to thank me, Miss Williams. If we get there and get your shoe box, then you can thank me."

She smiled and walked to the door, and I eyed her legs and the way she moved. "Tomorrow, then."

"Tomorrow," I said.

She stepped out of the office and shut the door behind her.

I counted about fifteen seconds, and then, no doubt to the surprise of my new client had she known, I immediately went to work.

I put on my hat and coat and went out, locking the door behind me. I took the steps two at a time, out to the chaos that was Scollay Square, and then I spotted her, heading up Tremont Street. I dodged more sailors and some loud, red-faced businessmen, the kind who had leather cases full of samples and liked to raise hell in big bad Boston before crawling back to their safe little homes in Maine or New Hampshire.

My client went around the corner, and I quickly lost her.

Damn.

I looked up and down the street, saw some traffic, more guys moving around, but not my client. A few feet away I stopped a man in a wheelchair, with a tartan blanket covering the stumps that used to be his legs. Tony Blawkowski, holding a cardboard sign: *HELP AN INJURED VET*. I went over and greeted him: "Ski."

"Yeah?" He was staring out at the people going by, shaking a cardboard coffee cup filled with coins.

"You see a young gal come this way?"

"Good lookin', small leather purse in her hands, hat on top of her pretty little head?"

"That's the one."

"Nope, didn't see a damn thing." He smiled, showing off yellow teeth.

I reached into my pocket, tossed a quarter in his cup.

"Well, that's nice, refreshin' my memory like that," Ski said. "Thing is, she came right by here, wigglin' that fine bottom of hers, gave me no money, the stuck-up broad, and then she got into a car and left."

Somehow the noise of the horns and the music from the burlesque hall seemed to drill into my head. "You sure?"

"Damn straight. A nice Packard, clean and shiny. It was parked there for a while, then she got in and left."

"You see who was in the Packard?"

"You got another quarter?"

I reached back into my pocket, and there was another clink as the coin fell into his cup. He laughed. "Nope. Didn't see who was in there or who was driving. They jus' left. That's all."

"All right, Ski. Tell you what, you see that Packard come back, you let me know, all right?"

"What's in it for me?"

I smiled. "Keeping your secret, for one."

He shook his head. "Bastard. You do drive a hard bargain."

"Only kind I got tonight."

I started to walk away, then looked back. As a couple of out-of-towners dropped some coins in Ski's cup, I thought about the sign. It was true, for Ski was an injured vet. He had been in the army, and one night, on leave here in town a couple of years ago, he got drunk out of his mind, passed out in front of a bar, and was run over by an MTA trolley, severing both legs.

Nice little story, especially the lesson it gave, for never accepting what you see on the surface.

About a half hour later, I was at the local district headquarters of the Boston Police Department, where I found Sergeant Francis Xavier O'Connor sitting behind a chest-high wooden desk, passing on whatever was considered justice in this part of town. There in the lobby area, the tile floor yellow and stained, two women in bright red lipstick, hands cuffed together, shared a cigarette on a wooden bench. O'Connor had a folded over copy of the *Boston American* in his hands, his face red and flush, and he glanced up at me as I approached the desk.

"Ah, Beantown's biggest dick," he said over half-glasses.

"Nice to see you too, sergeant. Thought you'd be spending some time up at your vacation spot on Conway Lake."

"Bah, the hell with you," O'Connor said. "What kind of trash are you lookin' for tonight?"

I leaned up against the desk, my wrists on the wooden edge. "What I'm looking for is right in front of me."

"Eh?"

"Quick question," I said. "Got a visit tonight from a young

lady, mid-twenties, said she was from Seattle, looking for some help. She told me she came here, talked to you, and somehow my name came up. Why's that?"

He grinned, bounced the edge of the folded newspaper against his chin. "Ah, I remember that little flower. Came sauntering in, sob story in one hand, a Greyhound bus ticket in the other, and she told me what kind of man she was lookin' for, and what the hell? I gave her your name and address. You should be grateful."

"More curious than grateful. Come on, Francis, answer the question. Why me?"

He leaned over, close enough so I could smell old onions coming from his breath. "Figure it out. Young gal had some spending money, spent it for some info . . . a name. And you know what? Her story sounded screwy enough that it might fuck over whoever decided to take her on as a client, and your name was first, second, and third on my list. Any more questions, dick?"

I stepped away from the desk. "Yeah. Your dad's nose still look like a lumpy potato after my dad finished him off?"

His face grew even more red. "Asshole, get out of my station."

The next evening I went into the Shamrock Fish & Tackle, off L Street in South Boston, near where I grew up. It was crowded as I moved past the rows of fishing tackle, rods, other odds and ends. Out in the back, smoking a cigar and nursing a Narragansett beer, Roddy Taylor looked up as I approached him. He had on a sleeveless T-shirt that had probably been white at one time, and khaki pants. He was mostly bald but tufts of hair grew from his thick ears.

"Corporal Sullivan, what are you up to tonight?"

"Looking to borrow an outboard skiff, if that's all right with you."

"Hell, of course."

"And stop calling me corporal."

He laughed and leaned back, snagged a key off a nail on the wall. He tossed it to me and I caught it with my right hand. "Number five."

"Okay, number five."

"How's your mom?" Roddy asked.

"Not good," I said. "She . . . well, you know."

He took a puff from his cigar. "Yeah. Still thinking your brother's coming home. Am I right?"

I juggled the key in my hand. "I'll bring it back sometime tonight."

"Best to your mom."

"You got it."

Outside I went to the backseat of my old Ford and took out a canvas gym bag. From the dirt parking lot I headed over to a dock and moved down the line of skiffs and boats, found the one with a painted number five on the side, and undid the lock. I tossed my gym bag in the open skiff, near the small fuel tank and the drain plug at the stern. I stood up and stretched. Overhead lights had come on, illuminating the near empty parking lot, the dock, and the line of moored boats.

She was standing at the edge of the dock. She still had her leather purse but the skirt had been replaced by slacks and flat shoes.

"Miss Williams," I said.

"Please," she said, coming across the dock. "Please call me Mandy."

"All right, Mandy it is."

She peered down at the skiff. "It looks so small."

"It's big enough for where we're going," I said.

"Are you sure?"

"I grew up around here, Miss—"

"Mandy."

"Mandy, I grew up around here." I looked about the water, at the lights coming on at the shoreline of Boston Harbor and the islands scattered out there at the beginnings of the Atlantic Ocean. "I promise you, I'll get you out and back again in no time."

She seemed to think about that for a moment, and nodded. Then she moved closer and gingerly put one foot into the boat, as I held her hand. Her hand felt good. "Up forward," I said. "Take the seat up forward."

My client clambered in and I followed. I undid the stern line and gently pushed us off, then primed the engine by using a squeeze tube from the small fuel tank. A flick of the switch and a couple of tugs with the rope starter, and the small Mercury engine burbled into life. We made our way out of the docks and toward the waters of the harbor, motoring into the coming darkness, my right hand on the throttle of the engine.

After about five minutes she turned and said, "Where are the life jackets?"

"You figuring on falling in?"

She had a brittle laugh. "No, not at all. I'd just like to know, that's all."

I motioned with my free hand. "Up forward. And nothing to worry about, Mandy. I boated out here before I went to grade school and haven't fallen in yet."

She turned into herself, the purse on her lap, and I looked

over at the still waters of the harbor. It was early evening, the water very flat, the smell of the salt air pretty good after spending hours and hours on Scollay Square. Off to the left, the north, were the lights of the airport, and out on the waters I could see the low shapes of the islands. Over to the right was the harbor itself, and the lights of the moored freighters.

One of the islands was now off to starboard and Mandy asked, "What island is that?"

"Thompson," I said.

"I see buildings there. A fort?"

I laughed. "Hardly. That's the home of the Boston Farm and Trades School."

"The *what* school?"

"Farm and Trades. A fancy name for a school for boys who get into trouble. Like a reform school. One last chance before you get sent off to juvenile hall or an adult prison."

She turned, and in the fading light I could make out her pretty smile. "Sounds like you know that place firsthand."

"Could have, if I hadn't been lucky."

Soon we passed Thompson and up ahead was a low-slung island with no lights. The wind shifted, carrying with it a sour smell.

"What in God's name is that?" Mandy asked.

"Spectacle Island. That's where the city dumps its trash. Lots of garbage up there, and probably the bodies of a few gangsters. Good place to lose something."

"You know your islands."

"Sure," I said. "They all have a story. All have legends. Indians, privateers, ghosts, pirates, buried treasure . . . everything and anything."

Now we passed a lighthouse, and I said, "Long Island,"

but Mandy didn't seem to care. There was another, smaller island ahead. "That's Gallops. You ready?" I asked.

"Yes," she replied, her voice strained. "Quite ready."

I ran the skiff aground on a bit of sandy beach and waded in the water, dragging a bowline up, tying it off some scrub brush. There was a dock just down the way, with a path leading up to the island, and by now it was pretty dark. From my gym bag I took out a flashlight and cupped the beam with my hand, making sure only a bit of light escaped.

"I want to make this quick, okay?"

She nodded.

"I asked around," I said. "I know where the barracks are. Do you happen to know where his bunk was located?"

"Next to a window overlooking the east, in the far corner. He always complained that the morning sun would hit his eyes and wake him up before reveille."

"All right," I said. "Let's go."

From the path near the dock, it was pretty easy going, much to my surprise. The place was deserted and there were no lights, but my own flashlight did a good job of illuminating the way. We headed along a crushed stone path; halfway there, something small and furry burst out of the brush, scaring the crap out of me and making Mandy cry out. She grabbed my free hand and wouldn't let it go—I didn't complain. It felt good, and she kept her hand in mine all the way up to the barracks.

A lot of the windows were smashed, and the door leading inside was hanging free from its hinges. We moved up the wide steps and gingerly stepped in. I flashed the light around. The roof had leaked and there were puddles of water on the floor. We went to the left, where there was a great open room stretching out into the distance. I slashed the light around again. Rusting frames for bunks were piled high in the corner, and there was an odd, musty smell to the place. Lots of old memories came roaring back, being in a building like this, taking in those old scents, of the soap and gun oil . . . and the smell of the men, of course.

I squeezed Mandy's hand and she squeezed back. Here we had all come, from all across the country, to train and to learn and to get ready to fight . . . and no matter what crap the RKO movies showed you, we were all scared shitless. It was a terrible time and place to come together, to know that so many of you would never return . . . torn up, blown up, shattered, burned, crushed, drowned. So many ways to die . . . and now to come back to what was called peace and prosperity and hustle and bustle and try to keep ahead. What a time.

"Let's go," I whispered, not sure why I was whispering. "I want to get out of here before someone spots our light."

"Yes," she whispered back, and it was like we were in church or something. I led my client down the way, our footsteps echoing off the wood, and I kept the light low, until we came to the far corner, the place where the windows looked out to the east, where a certain man rested in his bunk, the sun hitting his face every morning.

"Here," she whispered. "Shine the light over here."

She knelt down in the corner of the room, her fingers prying at a section of baseboard, and even though I half expected it, I was still surprised. The board came loose and Mandy cried out a bit; I lowered the flashlight and illuminated a small cavity.

"Hold on," I said, "you don't know what—"

But she didn't listen to me. She reached her right arm

down and rummaged around, murmuring, "Oh, Roger. Oh, my Roger."

Then she pulled her hand back, holding a box for Bass shoes, the damp cardboard held together with gray tape. She clasped the box against her chest and leaned over, silently weeping, I thought, her body shaking and trembling.

I gave her a minute or two, and then touched her shoulder. "Mandy, come on, we have to get out of here. And now."

And she got off her knees, wiped at her eyes, and with one hand held the cardboard box and her small leather purse against her chest.

Her other hand took mine, and wouldn't let go until we got back to the boat.

In the boat I pushed off and fired up the engine, and we started away from Gallops Island. The wind had come up some, nothing too serious, but there was a chop to the water that hadn't been there before. With the box in her lap, she turned and smiled, then leaned in toward me. I returned the favor and kissed her, and then kissed her again, and then our mouths opened and her hand squeezed my leg. "Oh, Billy . . . I didn't think it would work . . . I really didn't . . . Look, when we get back, we need to celebrate, okay?"

I liked her taste and her smell. "Sure. Celebrate. That sounds good."

But I kept looking at the water and kicked up the throttle some more.

It didn't seem to take too long, and as we motored back to the docks of the Shamrock Fish & Tackle, Mandy turned to me and started talking, about her life in Seattle, about her Roger, and about how she was ready to start a new life now that she had this box. I tried to ignore her chatter as we moved toward the dock, and when I looked up at the small parking lot, I noticed there was an extra vehicle there.

A Packard, parked underneath a street lamp.

As we drew close to the docks, doors to the Packard opened up and two men with hats and topcoats, their hands in their coats, stepped out.

Mandy was still chattering.

I worked the throttle, slipped the engine into neutral, and then reversed. The engine made a clunk-whine noise as I backed out of the narrow channel leading into the docks, and Mandy was jostled. "What the—"

"Hold on," I snapped, backing away even further. I shifted into neutral again, then forward, and finally sped away. Turning back, I saw the two guys return to the Packard and head out onto L Street. I immediately grabbed my flashlight and switched the engine off. We began drifting in the darkness.

Mandy gaped and asked, "Billy . . . what the hell is going on?"

"You tell me," I countered.

"I don't know what you mean."

"Mandy . . . what's in the box?"

"I told you," she said, her voice rising. "Souvenirs! Letters! Photos! Stuff that means so much to me . . ."

"And the guys in the Packard? Who are they? Friends of Roger who want to giggle over old photos of him in the army?"

"I don't know what you mean about—"

I pointed the flashlight in her face, flicked it on, startling her. I reached forward, snatched the damp box from her hands, sat back down. The boat rocked, a bit of spray hitting my arm.

"Hey!" she cried out, but now the box was in my lap.

I lowered the flashlight, seeing her face pursed and tight. "Let's go over a few things," I said. "You come into my office with a great tale, a great sob story. And you tell me you get hooked up with me because you just happened to run into one of the sleaziest in-the-bag cops on the Boston force, a guy who can afford a pricey vacation home on a New Hampshire lake on a cop's salary. And right after you leave my office, a sweet girl, far, far away from home, you climb into somebody's Packard. And now there's a Packard waiting for you at dockside. Hell of a coincidence, eh? Not to mention the closer we got to shore, the more you blathered at me, like you were trying to distract me."

She kept quiet, her hands now about her purse, firmly in her lap.

"Anything to say?" My client kept quiet. I held up the box. "What's in here, Mandy?"

Nothing.

"Mandy?"

I set the box back in my lap, tore away at the tape and damp cardboard, and the top lifted off easy enough. There was damp brown paper in the box, and the sound of smaller boxes moving against each other. I turned the big box over a bit, shone the light in. Little yellow cardboard boxes, about the size of small toothpaste containers, all bundled together. There were scores of them. I shuddered, took a deep breath. I knew what they were.

"Morphine," I said, looking her hard in the eye. "Morphine syrettes. Your guy . . . if there *was* a guy there, he wasn't training as a radioman. He was training as a medic. And he was stealing this morphine to sell later, once the war was over. Am I right? Who the hell are you, anyway?"

My client said, "What difference does it make? Look, I

had a job to do, to get that stuff off that island, easiest way possible, no fuss, no muss, and we did it. Okay? Get me to shore, you'll get . . . a finder's fee, a percentage."

I shook the box, heard the smaller boxes rattle. "Worth a lot of money, isn't it?"

She smiled. "You have no idea."

"But it was stolen. During wartime."

"So what?" Her voice now revealed a sharpness I hadn't heard before. "Guys went to war, some got killed, some figured out a way to score, to make some bucks . . . and the guys I'm with, they figured it was time to look out for themselves, to set something up for later. So there you go. Nice deal all around. Don't you want part of it, Billy? Huh?"

I shook the box again, fought to keep my voice even. "Ever hear of Bastogne?"

"Maybe, who knows, who cares."

"I know, and I care. That's where my brother was, in December 1944. Belgian town, surrounded by the Krauts. He took a chunk of shrapnel to the stomach. He was dying. Maybe he could have lived if he wasn't in so much pain . . . but the medics, they were low on morphine. They could only use morphine on guys they thought might live. So my brother . . . no morphine . . . he died in agony. Hours it took for him to die, because the medics were short on morphine."

Mandy said, "A great story, Billy. A very touching story. Look, you want a tissue or something?"

And moving quickly, she opened up her purse and took out a small, nickel-plated semiautomatic pistol.

"Sorry, Billy, but this is how it's going to be. You're going to give me back my box, you're going to take me back to the dock, and if you're a good boy, I'll make sure only a leg or an arm gets broken. How's that for a deal?"

I thought for a moment, now staring at a face I didn't recognize, and said, "I've heard better."

And I tossed the box and the morphine syrettes into the
dark waters.

She screamed and shouted something, and I was moving
quick, which was good, because she got off a shot that pounded
over my head as I ducked and grabbed something at the bottom of the boat, tugging it free, then dropped overboard. The
shock of the cold water almost made me open my mouth, but
I was more or less used to it. I came up coughing, splashing,
and my flashlight was still on the boat, still lit up, which made
it easy for me to see what happened next.

The skiff was rocking and filling with water as Mandy
moved to the rear, trying to get the engine started, I think, but
with her added weight at the stern, it quickly swamped and
flipped over, dumping her in. She screamed. She screamed
again. "Billy! Please! I can't swim! Please!"

I raised my hand, holding the drain plug to the rear of the
skiff, and let it go.

She floundered some more. Splashing. Yelling. Coughing.
It would be easy enough to get over there, calm her down, put
her in the approved life-saving mode, my arm about her, to
pull her safely to shore. So easy to do, for I could have easily
found her in the darkness by following the splashes and yells.

The yells. I had heard later, from someone in my brother's
platoon, how much he had yelled toward the end.

I moved some, was able to gauge where she was, out there
in the darkness.

And then I turned and swam in the other direction.

THE REWARD

BY STEWART O'NAN

Brookline

Sometimes Boupha honestly found them. She thought it was a gift. Her father said she wasn't so special—anybody could. He should know because it was his game; he'd been running it since he'd been driving a cab. After a while you developed an eye, like a hunter.

"American people don't see anything," he said. "People like us, we have to."

He'd taught her well, as he never tired of reminding her. Late August, when the college kids moved in, she watched the park. Winter she cruised the potholed lots behind the apartments on Jersey. In spring the long flats of Beacon beyond Kenmore were littered with the dead—worth just as much, and less trouble, besides the smell. In her trunk she kept garbage bags and rubber gloves, an aerosol can of Oust.

Each season brought a new crop, that was the genius of it. Her father was the one who'd realized the possibilities. Now that he could no longer drive, Boupha used his badge, working twelve-hour shifts to pay his hospital bills. After all his talk about keeping her eyes open, he'd been going fifty on Storrow Drive in the rain when he rear-ended a stopped tow truck. His head bent the steering wheel. The wheel could be fixed but not her father. The doctors had saved his life so he could lie in a special bed and watch TV. "Boupha!" he called when he needed anything. "Boupha!" Their apartment wasn't large enough to escape his voice. He'd had a sly sense of humor before the accident, a con man's easy charm. Now her smallest mistake sent him into a rage. She hated leaving him alone because sometimes, for no reason, he screamed. The upstairs neighbors had complained.

On his best days, he obsessed over money and cigarettes. He didn't care about food or temple anymore. His friend Pranh no longer visited.

"How much you make today?" he asked when she came home, already reaching for his Newports. Every dollar, every pack was an offering to him.

Like driving, so much of the game was being in the right place. That night she wasn't even looking. She'd dropped a silent fare at Beth Israel and stopped at the Store 24 on Beacon when the shepherd limped out of an alley directly into her path, as if it didn't see her.

Even with the shadows she could tell it was an older male, rheumy-eyed and white around the snout. Its haunches were matted black and it was hobbling so badly that she thought it had been hit. One of her father's cardinal rules was that a hurt animal wasn't worth the trouble. She'd once found a cat on Park Drive with its back legs smashed, writhing and spitting. It had no collar, so it was worthless, but Boupha couldn't leave it in the street. As she tried to slide it to the curb on a pizza box, it snarled and clawed her arm, opening three beading lines she now wore as scars. "I tell you," her father had said, "but you're too smart, you don't want to listen."

Normally strays shied away, distrustful of people, but the shepherd just waddled along ahead of her. Its back was slick with blood; it shone under the streetlights. She was almost beside her car. Thinking of the cat lashing out, she stopped.

The dog stopped and looked back as if they were going for a walk and she needed to catch up. Its tag glinted.

She had treats in the glove compartment, a leash with a muzzle. She could quote her father back to him: older dogs were worth more. The owners had more invested in them.

But the blood. The blood was a problem.

The dog turned to watch her open the passenger door, cocking his head.

"Hey. I've got something for you. Here you go."

She tossed him a treat. He waddled over and nosed it, keeping his eyes on her the whole time. Finally he took the biscuit, crunching it with his head lowered.

"Good boy, yes."

The second one she dropped halfway between them. This time he didn't hesitate.

"That's a good dog," she said, and squatted down to show she was no threat. With the leash behind her back, she set a treat on the sidewalk right in front of her.

As he came closer, he hunched lower and lower until he lay down and rolled on his side, panting, his tongue flopping out of his mouth.

"It's all right, you're okay," she said, and hooked the leash to the ring on his collar.

She pushed the treat toward him and he rolled and took it and got to his feet, chomping. She waited till he was finished to pet him. His tag said his name was Edgar and he belonged to the Friedmans. The phone number was a Brookline exchange, a point in her favor.

He was still panting, so she took the bowl from the trunk and gave him some water. As he lapped, she inspected his haunch, pouring the rest of the bottle over it. She rinsed most of the blood off but there wasn't enough light to see where it was coming from.

"I know it hurts, Edgar," she said, drying him with an old

towel, but he didn't seem to mind. He stood still for her as if he was getting a bath. Maybe he was senile, or maybe he was just good-natured.

He looked good enough. She laid a trash bag and another towel across the backseat for him and drove straight home. It took only five minutes this time of night, but in the lot, when she opened the back door, his rear was matted again and the towel was bloody.

Later she realized this was where she should have cut him loose, but she'd already made her decision, and the possibility never crossed her mind. She thought she'd saved him. He had the tag, the tag had the number. That was the game. The only thing she was worried about was her father.

She couldn't lie to him. The dog didn't want to go in the cage, and there was blood on her shirt, blood on her arms. She gave him his cigarettes first.

"I don't believe you," he said. "What do I tell you, and you do this."

"I'm going to call them," she said, but when she did, there was no answer.

Edgar was bleeding in the cage, and she had to make dinner.

"Get it out of here," her father said. "What are you waiting for?"

She called the Friedmans again while he was eating. She thought it was wrong. She should at least be getting a machine.

She coaxed Edgar out of the cage and lifted him into the bathtub the way she did her father, using the flexible hose to wash his haunch. As she scrubbed him, something sharp cut her palm.

She looked at the hole in her rubber glove as if it couldn't have happened, but the blood was already welling up.

"Shit."

"What is it?" her father called.

"Nothing."

She held Edgar still and gingerly parted his fur. Poking from a lipped gash in his gray skin was the broken blade of a steak knife.

She needed the pliers to ease it out. He didn't growl as she cleaned and dressed the wound. She used extra butterflies and checked on him every few minutes to make sure he wasn't digging at it. He didn't like the cage, so she'd put down a blanket in a corner and given him a few toys. He lay with a stuffed Tigger between his crossed paws, licking the head as if it were a pup.

"I don't know why anyone would do that to you," she said, stroking him. "You're a good boy."

"Call them again," her father said.

She had the number right, they just weren't home. She had their address. Tomorrow she'd swing by and see if they'd put up posters. She wondered how long it had been.

In the middle of the night she woke to her father calling for her and the dog barking. Edgar must have nosed the door open, because he was in the middle of her father's room, his front legs braced, his fangs bared. It was like the two of them were arguing.

"Go!" Boupha shouted, clapping, and Edgar slunk away.

"Keep him away from me!" her father screamed, wild-eyed. "He tried to bite me!"

"I'll close your door. That way you'll be safe."

"Don't leave me alone!"

"I'm right here, Pa," she said, patting his arm. "I'm not going anywhere."

In the morning he was calmer, but he wanted the dog gone. Now, today.

Edgar's bleeding had stopped, the blood crusted darkly around the butterflies. The way the game worked, the longer you held on to them, the greater your reward, but her father made that impossible. She called the Friedmans, and when no one answered, she clipped Edgar to his leash and took him to Brookline.

The address on his tag belonged to a leafy side street. It was the kind of neighborhood she could never afford, with neat lawns and hedges and gardens. As she slowed, searching for the number, Edgar sat up in the backseat as if he knew where they were going.

The Friedmans' was a white frame house with baskets of geraniums hanging from the porch. Behind her, Edgar huffed and scratched at the window.

"Let me stop the car first."

When she opened the door, he shot across the yard and up the steps, trailing his leash, a burst of energy that made her think he was feeling better. He waited, facing the doorknob, as if she had the key.

She took the leash in hand and rang the bell, then stepped back, standing straight, her chin held high. Americans liked you to look them in the eye so they knew you were telling the truth. In this case Boupha was, but out of habit she prepared the details of her story, like an actor about to take the stage. As proof, she would show the Friedmans the Band-Aid on her palm. She wouldn't ask for a reward, would turn it down at first. Only when they insisted would she accept it, thanking them in turn for their generosity, and everyone would be happy.

After standing there a minute, Boupha pressed the door-bell again and heard it chime inside—*bing-bong.*

"They're probably all out looking for you," she said, scratching Edgar's head.

She was about to knock when a voice called, "Can I help you?"

It came from the porch next door, from an older lady with puffy white hair and red lipstick. She wore a flowered apron over a powder-blue sweat suit. In one gloved hand, drawn like a weapon, she held a spade.

"I'm looking for the Friedmans," Boupha said.

"I'm sorry, the Friedmans aren't here. They're both gone."

"I think I found their dog."

"Is that Edgar?" the woman said, craning as if she couldn't see him. "I thought the police took him."

Just the mention of them made Boupha want to excuse herself.

"Wait right there." The woman tottered down the stairs and across the yard. "Oh God, it *is* Edgar."

Boupha went right into her story. When she described finding the blade, the woman covered her mouth with both hands.

"Oh dear, you don't know, do you? You didn't hear what happened to them?"

"No."

"I thought everyone knew. It was all over the TV. There were reporters tromping all over my yard. I refused to talk to them. I told them they could go dig up their dirt somewhere else. It was a tragedy, that's all. God forgives everything, I have to believe that. The people I feel sorry for are the children."

"What happened?"

She really didn't want to talk about it. The woman would just give Boupha the basics—she could get them from the paper anyway.

Last Wednesday, in the middle of the night, Mr. Friedman,

who was having serious health problems, took a kitchen knife and stabbed Mrs. Friedman—who was having even more serious health problems—many times. Then Mr. Friedman stabbed himself, once, in the neck (the woman gestured with the spade). He survived, she died, which the woman guessed was better than the other way around, but it was still horrible. They were both such nice people. Mrs. Friedman had been president of the Hadassah.

"I'm sorry," Boupha said.

"It's no mystery. He couldn't take care of her anymore, that was all. He was afraid."

"You said there are children." She petted Edgar as if to show how good he was.

"They're long gone. They wanted to get as far away as possible from this mess, and I don't blame them. I don't have the slightest idea how to get ahold of them. You might try the police. It's a shame. He always had such a sweet disposition for a shepherd. I'd take him in a second if I wasn't allergic."

"Is there anyone around here who could?"

The woman shrugged and shook her head as if there was nothing anyone could do.

Boupha knew what her father would do. He'd leave the dog sitting on the porch and drive away. Boupha thought she could have done that too, if the woman wasn't standing there. Maybe later she could come back and tie him to a tree in the backyard—but how long would he be there, and who would find him? She might as well drive over to Brighton and drop him off at animal control.

She thanked the woman and—finally resorting to treats again—convinced Edgar to get back in the cab. In the rear-view mirror, he watched his old home go, and she wondered if, that night, he'd tried to protect Mrs. Friedman, or whether it had already been too late and he was just lucky to escape. The way he acted on the porch, she wasn't sure he understood what had happened. Had he expected them to be there waiting for him?

He was old, and hurt, and maybe he couldn't imagine that great of a change.

When she let him out in their parking lot, she noticed bloody pawprints on the seat. He'd probably opened the cut running across the yard.

"I tell you!" her father shouted. "You get rid of him! Boupha!"

She closed the bathroom door to tend to Edgar, but the butterflies were fine. In the other room, her father raged.

"Stop!" she finally shouted. "I can hear you. Everyone can hear you. I'll get rid of him when he's better. Right now he's sick."

"That's why you need to get rid of him! You're not a doctor!"

She wasn't, and she really needed to be. That night, as she was falling asleep, Edgar got up from his corner, padded to a spot in front of her closet, and squatted. The puddling noise woke her.

"No!" she yelled. "Bad!"

Fearing diarrhea, she turned on the light and saw he was unleashing a bloody stream. He looked over at her guiltily as it gushed out of him onto the carpet.

She jumped up in just her T-shirt and dragged him into the kitchen so he would go on the linoleum, because he wasn't done, but that only made a bigger mess.

"What's happening?" her father shouted.

"He's sick."

"I tell you that already."

Someone upstairs stomped on the floor.

"Shut up!" Boupha yelled at the ceiling.

Bomp, bomp, bomp!

"Boupha! Listen to me! Get rid of it!"

In the whole city, the only animal hospital that was open was in Brookline. She laid down towels, knowing they wouldn't do any good. He couldn't stop. She couldn't stop it. Her father was right, she wasn't a doctor, and when she parked by the sliding doors and carried the dog inside, her sopping T-shirt sticking to her skin, there was nothing the doctor could do either.

She paid them to take care of him, a week's worth of tips.

"What I tell you?" her father said. "You don't listen. Stupid."

The next morning she cleaned the carpet, going over the spot with Resolve and a scrub brush. She threw out the toys and blankets and folded the cage away. She took the car to the self-wash, using the rubber gloves and Oust one last time.

She worked. She drove. She bought her father cigarettes and listened to him cough. In the night he summoned her. "Boupha!" he called. "Boupha!" And sometimes, as she made her way through the darkened kitchen, she imagined the knives piled in the silverware drawer, and wondered how strong or how weak you would have to be to use them. Not very, she thought.

THE CROSS-EYED BEAR

BY JOHN DUFRESNE

Southie

Father Tom Mulcahy can't seem to get warm. He's wearing his bulky cardigan sweater over his flannel pajamas over his V-neck T-shirt. He's got fleece-lined cordovan slippers on over his woolen socks and an afghan folded over his lap. The radiator is clanging and hissing in the corner, and he's still shivering. He tugs his watch cap over his ears, wipes his runny nose with a tissue. He stares at the bed against the wall and longs for the sleep of the dead. The window rattles. The weather people expect eighteen to twenty inches from the storm. He sips his Irish whiskey, swallows the other half of the Ativan, opens Meister Eckhart, and reads how all of our suffering comes from love and affection. He slips the venomous letter into the book to mark his page. The red numerals on the alarm clock seem to float in their black box. He sees his galoshes tucked under the radiator, the shaft of the right one bent to the floor. He's so tired he wonders if the droopy galosh might be a sign from God. Then he smiles and takes another sip of whiskey.

He lifts a corner of the curtain, peeks out on the driveway below, and sees fresh footprints leading to the elementary school. Probably Mr. O'Toole, the parish custodian, up early to clear the walk, an exercise in futility, it seems to Father Tom. The snow swirls, and the huge flakes look like black moths in the spotlight over the rectory porch. How new the world seems like this, all the clutter and debris mantled in white. He looks at the school and remembers the childhood exhilaration of snow days. Up early, radio on, listening to 'BZ, waiting for Carl De Suze to read the cancellation notices: *"No school in Arlington, Belmont, and Beverly. No school, all schools, Boston . . ."* In the years before his brother died, Tom would wake Gerard with the wicked good news, and the pair of them would pester their mom for cocoa and then snuggle under blankets on the couch and watch TV while she trudged off to work at Filene's. They'd eat lunch watching Big Brother Bob Emery, and they'd toast President Eisenhower with their glasses of milk while Big Brother's phonograph played "Hail to the Chief." Maybe if Gerard had lived, if they'd taken him to the hospital before it was too late, maybe then their dad would not have lost heart and found the highway.

Father Tom woke up this morning—well, yesterday morning now—woke up at 5:45 to get ready to celebrate the 6:30 Mass. He opened his eyes and saw the intruder sitting in the rocking chair. Father Tom said, "Who are you?"

"I'm with the *Globe.*"

"Mrs. Walsh let you in?"

"I let myself in."

"What's going on?"

The man from the *Globe* tapped his cigarette ash into the cuff of his slacks.

"No smoking in the room, Mr. . . . ?"

"Hanratty."

"I'm allergic."

"Does the name Lionel Ferry mean anything to you?"

Father Tom found himself accused of sexual abuse by a man who claimed to have been molested and raped while he was an altar boy here at St. Cormac's. Thirty-some years ago. A reticent boy whom Father Tom barely thinks about anymore, not really, now a troubled adult looking for publicity and an easy payday from the archdiocese, needing an excuse to explain his own shabby and contemptible life, no doubt. Out for a little revenge against the Church for some fancied transgression. Father Tom had no comment for this Mr. Hanratty. And he has no plans to read the morning papers. But he does know they'll come for him, the press, the police, the cardinal's emissaries. His life as he knew it is over. Already the monsignor has asked him not to say Mass this morning—no use giving the disaffected an easy target.

He never did a harmful thing to any child, but he will not be believed. He prays to Jesus, our crucified Lord, to St. Jude, and to the Blessed Virgin. Father Tom trusts that God would not give him a burden he could not bear. He puts out the reading lamp. He stuffs earplugs in his ears, shuts his eyes, and covers them with a sleep mask. He feels crushed with fatigue, but his humming brain won't shut down. He keeps hearing that Paul Simon song about a dying constellation in a corner of the sky. The boy in the bubble and all that. *These are the days of . . .* And then unfamiliar faces shape themselves out of the caliginous murk in front of his closed eyes and morph into other faces, and soon he is drifting in space and shimmering like numerals on a digital clock, and then he's asleep. In his dream he's a boy again, and he's sitting with Jesus on a desolate hill overlooking Jerusalem. It's very late, and the air, every square inch of it, is purple. Jesus weeps. Tom knows what Jesus knows, that soon Jesus will be betrayed. Jesus wipes His eyes with the sleeve of His robe and says, "You always cheer me up, Thomas," and He tickles Tom in the ribs. Tom laughs, tucks his elbows against his sides, and rolls away. "Do you like that,

Thomas? Do you?" Tom likes it, but he tells Jesus to stop so he can breathe. "Stop, please, or I'll wet my pants!" But Jesus won't stop.

Father Tom wakes up when the book drops to the floor. He takes off the sleep mask, picks up the letter, unfolds it, and reads in the window light. *I'll slice off your junk and stuff it down your throat, you worthless piece of shit. I'll drench you with gasoline and strike the match that sends you to hell.*

While he's waiting for the monsignor to finish up in the bathroom, Father Tom considers the painting he's been staring at all his life. It hung in the front hall of the family's first-floor apartment on L Street when he was a boy, and he was sure it must have been called *Sadness* or *Gloom*. His parents had no idea what it was called. The painting was a gift from an Irish cousin on his mother's side was all they knew. One of the O'Sullivans from Kerry. Now it hangs on the wall above Father Tom's prie-dieu. As a boy he saw this ragged, bare-foot woman sitting on a rock in the middle of an ocean with her eyes blindfolded and her head bandaged and chained to a wooden frame that he assumed to be an instrument of torture, but turned out to be a lyre, of all things, and the rock was really the world itself, and the title was actually and inexplicably *Hope*. He's been trying to understand the aspiration, the anticipation in this somber and forlorn study in hazy blues and pale greens all his life. Hope is blind? Does that even make sense? The lyre has only one string. So the music is broken. The dark sky is starless. All he's ever felt looking at the picture is melancholy and desolation. Hopelessness. Is that it? If you are without desire, you are free?

He hears the bathroom door open and Monsignor McDermott descend the creaky staircase. The bathroom reeks of Listerine and bay rum aftershave. He folds the monsignor's pearl-handled straight razor and puts it by the shaving brush and mug. He starts the shower and lets the room steam and warm while he shaves. He stares in the mirror and wonders what people see when they look at him. He cuts himself in the little crease beside his lip and applies a tear of toilet paper to the bubble of blood. He looks at his face and sees his father's blue eyes and his mother's weak chin. He removes the toilet paper and dabs the cut with a styptic pencil. Gerard was the handsome one.

Mrs. Walsh, bless her heart, has already brewed the coffee and filled his cup. "Will it be eggs and toast, Father?"

"Just coffee this morning, Mary." He stirs his coffee, lays the spoon in the saucer. "The monsignor left for Mass already, I see." For just a second there, Father Tom forgot that today is not like other days. "I never did what that man said, you know."

"That's between you and the Lord, Father. It's no business of mine." She walks to the sink and peers out the window. "Sixteen inches already, and no sign of a letup. There'll be snow on the ground till Easter."

"I can't even remember the boy very clearly."

"He was one of your favorites, Father. Altar boy, he was. Tim Griffin's nephew. You called him 'Train.' He had the vocation, you used to say."

"But didn't become a priest."

"Became a drunk and a burden to his dear mother, may her soul rest in peace." Mrs. Walsh sets the dishcloth to dry on the radiator and straightens the braided rug by the stove, a rug she made herself thirty-some years ago from her husband's and children's discarded clothing. There's Himself's blue oxford shirt right there and little Mona's corduroy jumper. When she sees the shirt, she sees her dear Aidan in it and his gray suit and red tie on their honeymoon on Nantasket Beach. "There have been other accusations, Father. Other men have come forward."

"I did nothing except be kind to those boys, give them the love and attention they didn't get at home. I never—"

The doorbell chimes. Mrs. Walsh says, "That'll be Mr. Markey from the cardinal's office. He'll be wanting a word with you." She walks to the front door and adds over her shoulder, "He's a merciful Lord, Father."

Mr. Markey unsnaps his earflaps and takes off his storm hat. He holds it by the visor and slaps it against his leg, then hangs it on a peg and toes off his shearling boots. He hands his gloves and scarf to Mrs. Walsh and hangs his wool car coat on the hall tree, claps his hands together, and rubs them. He takes Mrs. Walsh by the shoulders and plants a noisy kiss on her forehead. "And how's my favorite colleen today?"

Mrs. Walsh blushes. "Enough of the blarney, Mr. Markey."

Mr. Markey holds out his hand to Father Tom. "Francis X. Markey." They shake hands. Mr. Markey points to the parlor. "Care to join me, Father?"

Father Tom sits on the edge of the sofa behind the coffee table, his hands folded on his knees. Mr. Markey drops into the upholstered armchair, leans his head back against the antimacassar, and runs his fingers through his hair. "I gave the monsignor five bucks and told him to get a forty-five-minute coffee at Dunkin' Donuts. It's the only thing open between here and the expressway." He leans forward. "You know why I'm here."

"I've been threatened, Mr. Markey." Father Tom slides the vicious letter across the coffee table.

Mr. Markey leans forward and reads it, steeples his fingers, and brings his hands to his face. "It won't be the last, I would guess. I should make one thing clear, Father. I don't care what you did or didn't do. I don't particularly care what happens to you. I don't care *about* you in any but the most Christianable way. I care about Holy Mother the Church."

"I didn't do what I've been accused of."

"You're up to your neck in shit, my friend." Mr. Markey walks to the French doors and closes them, then turns back to Father Tom. "You attended O'Connell Seminary, am I right?"

"I did."

"Yes, you did. You guys had a regular fuck show going over there, didn't you?"

"I don't have to listen to this."

"Yes, you do. I'm the only guy who can keep you out of Concord." Mr. Markey takes a handful of Skittles from the bowl on the coffee table and eats a few. "You do not want to go to prison."

"I'm innocent. I won't go to prison."

Mr. Markey smiles and shakes his head. "They'll put you in protective custody, of course. What you need to understand, however, is that the guards are scarier than the inmates when it comes to pedophiles. They'll piss in your food, shit in your bunk, and they'll sodomize you with a control baton if you complain. They'll degrade you in every way they can. And then one day while you're playing cribbage with another kiddie diddler, the guards will turn away when some trusty goes after you with a lead pipe."

Father Tom puts his head in his hands. He takes a deep breath and sits back, stares at the ceiling. He hears Mrs. Walsh whispering—her prayers, no doubt—as she climbs the stairs. "Why has His Eminence sent you here, Mr. Markey?"

"I make problems go away." He shows Father Tom his handful of Skittles, rubs his palms together, holds out two fists and says, "Which hand has the candy?"

"The left."

Mr. Markey opens his empty left hand and then his empty right hand. He turns his palms to show he's not hiding anything. "Do you remember a priest named Dan Caputo?"

"Died last year. Had a parish in JP and did all that social justice work. 'Speak truth to power,' and all that—he was an inspirational leader."

"But he had a secret, as so many of us do. The cops found his battered corpse in an alley in Chinatown, his pants down to his ankles, a cock ring on his dick, and what would prove to be semen on his lips. When they checked his ID and found out who he was, they called the cardinal, who called me."

"I didn't hear about any of this."

"Exactly. We got rid of the porn magazines and videos in his car. He died a hero." Mr. Markey sits in the armchair and looks at Father Tom. "The Catholic Workers named their new place after him. The Father Dan Caputo House of Hospitality." He laughs. "Nothing is ever what it seems to be, Father." He reaches in his pocket. "Weather alert." He takes out his BlackBerry. "This event has all the makings of a Storm of the Century." He reads his text message. "Calling for three feet inside 128." He puts the BlackBerry away. "Now this is what we're going to do. First, I'm going to offer our Mr. Ferry a handsome settlement in exchange for a signed statement admitting that he has been lying about the molestations due to his profound depression and anxiety. He'll agree to check himself into a mental health clinic; you'll be reassigned to a desk job at the chancery for the time being, and in a while this aggravation will be forgotten."

"It's in the papers."

"You'll do a press conference at which you'll graciously and humbly accept Mr. Ferry's apology and forgive him."

"And if he doesn't agree to your conditions?"

"That would suggest that he is a man of principle. But a penniless alcoholic, we both know, cannot afford principles."

"But if he surprises you, then we go to trial and I'm exonerated."

"Neither necessary nor desirable." Mr. Markey walks to the fireplace and leans against the mantle. "Let me ask your opinion, Father, about this epidemic of predatory priests. Not you, of course. The guilty ones like Geoghan and Shanley. That lot. And Father Gale over here at St. Monica's. The priesthood turns out to be a good place to hide in plain sight. Am I right?"

"I wouldn't call it—"

"Six hundred and fifteen million dollars the Church in the States paid out just last year. That makes two billion total. Fourteen thousand felonies by forty-five hundred pedophile priests. And it's only the tip of the iceberg, believe me." He squats and warms his hands over the fire. "I have a theory, for what it's worth." He moves his left hand into the flame and leaves it there. "A theory of arrested development."

"You'll burn yourself."

"You go to the seminary out of high school, and it's all paid for. You graduate and get your parish assignment—no chasing down leads, no job interviews." He pulls his hand out of the flame and examines it. "Along with the assignment comes food, clothing, and shelter, a salary, a woman to cook, clean up after you, and do your laundry. You get a professional allowance, health insurance, and a pension. You snap on the Roman collar, and you have instant respect without having earned it."

"That's unfair."

"The Church stifles your emotional growth. You're a boy called *Father*. Not just you personally, Father. All of you."

"Are you finished?"

"Then there's the disagreeable issue of celibacy. Troublesome, am I right? Me, if I can't release a few times a week, Jesus, I'm impossible to live with. Sure, you can masturbate and remain celibate and sane, but jacking off's a sin, so what to do?"

"Pray."

"You can pray away a boner?"

"One chooses to remain chaste, Mr. Markey. It's a sacrifice, not a curse."

Mr. Markey puts his hands behind his head and shrugs his shoulders. "But why little boys? That's what I wonder, and then I think, yes, of course, arrested development. If you're a boy yourself, you're comfortable among other boys, and you also know an abused boy would never say anything about sucking your cock for fear the other kids would call him a fag. Shame keeps him quiet. Am I getting warm, Father?"

"You think you know me, but you don't."

"Thomas Aloysius Mulcahy, born February 15, 1948, at Mass General, second son to Brian, postal worker, and Kathleen, née O'Sullivan, Mulcahy. Attended St. Cormac's Grammar School and South Boston High; B student, perfect attendance in eleventh grade. You had mumps, chicken pox, measles, and rubella. You wore corrective glasses and corrective shoes. Your beloved brother Gerard died of spinal meningitis in 1958, and your dad blamed himself, drank more heavily, and abandoned the family six months later. So there you were at ten, alone with a hysterical mother and bereft of affection."

Father Tom closes his eyes and sees himself lying on the floor by his mother's locked bedroom door, crying, not knowing if she was also dead. He feels Mr. Markey's hand on his shoulder and opens his eyes, wipes them.

"So you understood just how vulnerable boys who'd lost their dads were. They needed the love and guidance of an older man, and you reached out to them."

"You're making compassion sound obscene."

"You took them for ice cream, to Fenway, to the beach. Their mothers were so grateful. You were a savior. Lionel even thought you were using him to woo his mom. And, of course, with you being a priest, he was confused."

"You spoke with him?"

"Last night. He's still living in his mom's place on I Street." Mr. Markey stared out the window at the howling storm. "He said you took him to the movies."

"I took many boys to many movies."

"You bought popcorn, buttered popcorn. 'Butted,' he said. 'Hut butted pupcon,' and you held the box on your lap, and when he reached in for a handful, your fingers touched, and you let the touch linger. He said you licked the 'buttah' off his fingers—"

"He's lying."

"That could be. Or it could be false memories. That happens. But let me ask you this. Has any priest ever confessed abuse to you?"

"If any had, I wouldn't tell you."

"What would you do if Father X told you he boinked all the altos in the boys' choir?"

"I'd grant him absolution if he were contrite and determined not to sin again."

"That's it?"

"*If thy brother trespass against thee, rebuke him; and if he repent, forgive him.*"

"*Forgive, and ye shall be forgiven.*"

"I might also suggest counseling, therapy, prayer, and avoiding the near occasion to sin."

Mr. Markey picks up a copy of *The Pilot* off the coffee table and reads. "*Cardinal Law Appointed Archpriest at Vatican Basilica.*" He shakes his head, rolls the paper and slaps it against his leg. "Our ex-cardinal here once accused a six-year-old boy of negligence and culpability in his own repeated rapes. Under oath!" He drops the paper onto the coffee table. "I can't shake this paranoid fantasy I have of a fellowship of child-molesting priests all going to confession to one another, forgiving one another, and moving on as if nothing ever happened."

"One would need sincere contrition."

"They confess; they are contrite; they are forgiven." Mr. Markey checks his watch. "I'm going to need to speak with the monsignor alone. Maybe you should visit the church and pray for strength and guidance. By the time we see you again, everything should be taken care of." Mr. Markey puts his hand on the back of Father Tom's neck and squeezes. He pulls Father Tom's head toward his own until their foreheads touch. "Trust me."

Father Tom feels a hot current of pain buzz through his skull like his head's attached to a live electrical wire, but he's rigid, shaken, and speechless, and he can't pull away.

Father Tom lights a votive candle and prays for courage and understanding. He's always savored his time alone in a dark church where he feels hidden away. As a boy he'd arrive at 5 or 6 every Saturday morning, sit beneath the stained-glass window of the Last Supper, and pray the rosary. He wanted

God to know that he was no Sunday Catholic; he was a boy God could count on, a soldier of Christ. Father Tom genuflects, walks to the pew beneath the Last Supper, and sits. The world seems far away. He remembers asking God to make him either dead or invisible. Dead he'd be with Jesus and Gerard; invisible he'd be alone.

He looks up at the window. Jesus has a mole under His right eye. The beloved John has his head on his arm and his arm on the table. His eyes are shut, and he's smiling like he's tasted the honeyed love of his Lord. The apostle Thomas stands behind the others, and all you see is his single wide eye peering above the heads at Jesus, the way Gerard's single eye peered above the hem of the blanket on the couch when he ran his foot along Tom's leg. "Quit it, Gerard, or I'll call Mom!"

When Gerard lay in his coma at the hospital, the nuns from St. Cormac's took up residence in his room and kept a twenty-four-hour vigil. They fussed and prayed over him. Sister Brigid saw the Angel Gabriel at the foot of Gerard's bed, weeping. Gerard was a saint, the nuns were certain. The ones He loves best, God takes first. When Gerard died in his mother's arms, the nuns hung framed photos of Gerard in every classroom alongside the president and the Pope. Then the stories of Gerard's sanctity started, how he had healed a starling's broken wing with just a touch, how he could be both in church and in school simultaneously, how he could smell the presence of sin, how the statue of the Virgin Mary on the altar had wept at the moment of Gerard's passing.

What Father Tom will admit to if they ask—because it's pretty normal anyway—is that there are two selves in him. There's the self you see, the Father Tom he wants to be, the he who is pastoral, devout, compassionate, prudent . . . and what else? Vulnerable? Yes. And washed in the blood of the Lamb. And this is the bona fide Father Tom Mulcahy. And then there is the sinner, the carnal scoundrel who is impulsive, selfish, devious, and insatiable, a wolf inside who knows the secret of Father Tom's loneliness and hunger, and who would, if he could, twist Father Tom's selfless love and earnest affection into something loathsome and viperous. Father Tom will admit, this is to say, that he is indeed human and flawed, no better than they. And he'll explain to them his obsessive vigilance and tenacity in the battle with his pernicious other, and how he has always vanquished the interloping demon and has done so at a staggering price.

One day after sledding and making snow angels, he and Gerard built a snowman in the small backyard, and his brother took the carrot for the nose and stuck it down there and made it a weenie and told Tom to get down on his knees and eat it. He wouldn't, so Gerard pushed his face into the snow and sat on his head until Tom couldn't breathe, and he was terrified and his mother wasn't here to save him.

He hears a noise, like someone dropped a hymnal, but when he looks around, he sees no one. He says, "Mr. O'Toole?" and hears his voice echo. He listens to the howling wind and to his beating heart. And then he hears his sobbing mother say, *Why Gerard, dear God?* They are in the hospital and Tom is in a corner, peering past the nuns at his mother, prostrate on his dead brother's bed. *Why the beautiful one?* she says.

Father Tom prays for wisdom, guidance, and deliverance. He'll do God's will, and if God wants him to suffer unjustly, then so be it. But he's done with waiting. He'll speak with this Judas, this traducer, this Lionel Ferry, and give him a chance to confess his lies and to accept God's grace into his heart.

When Father Tom enters the sacristy, he's surprised by a

man in a cumbersome green snow suit standing in a puddle of melting snow. "Mr. O'Toole?" Father Tom says. A black balaclava covers most of the man's face. His mustache is white with ice, and his glasses are opaque with fog. This man, who is apparently not Davy O'Toole, who is, Father Tom realizes, several inches shorter than the custodian, has a snowball in his left hand, which he lobs to Father Tom. When Father Tom catches the ball against his chest, the man swings what must be a club and strikes him on the side of his face, and he drops to the floor. His skull is shattered, he's certain, but it doesn't hurt. He hears the squeak of footsteps, hears the church door open, squeal, and slam shut. After several minutes, he opens the one eye that will, touches his face, and feels the drilling pain. His left ear is ringing.

Father Tom holds a handful of numbing snow over his swollen eye, presses the buzzer, and waits. He kicks aside some drifted snow and forces the storm door open. He knocks on the inside front door twice and then *shave-and-a-haircut.* A voice says, "Come in if you're beautiful." Father Tom drops the snow from his eye, shakes off as much snow as he can from his coat and slacks, steps inside the unlit parlor, and lets his eye adjust. "Hello!" He can see his breath. He can make out a sofa and a sleeping bag spread on the floor. He hears, "Be right with you. Gotta drain the lizard."

The parlor is spare, grim, disordered, and in need of a good airing out and thorough cleaning. The flock wallpaper is peeling and water-stained. Next to the sleeping bag is a white plastic lawn chair stacked with magazines. There's a small TV on the floor and a bookcase crammed with videotapes in black boxes. He hears, "Make yourself at home." He steps around pizza boxes—pepperoni and sausage, or are those mouse droppings?—and piles of funky clothing and sits in an old wooden kitchen chair with a slat missing from the backrest. He notices an unframed paint-by-number portrait of Pope John Paul II hung over the light switch by the closed door to what had been Lionel's bedroom. He sees those eyes that follow you around the room.

Lionel enters cradling a bottle of vodka. He's wearing a waist-length leather jacket with an extravagant fur collar, black patent leather shoes, and no shirt. His khaki chinos have been pissed in.

"Train?"

"Tommy Gun!"

"What's happened to you?"

"That's what we called you behind your back."

"You don't have to live like this."

"Your eye?"

"I fell."

Lionel flops onto the couch. "I've been expecting you."

"You have?"

"For years." He drinks.

"We need to talk."

Lionel pats the sofa cushion. "Come sit with me."

"I'm fine here."

"I won't bite." He smiles. "I insist."

Father Tom moves to the sofa. "Did you write me a letter?"

"I never mailed it." Lionel touches Father Tom's arm. "I forgive you, Father. But I can't forget. That's the difference between me and God."

"I think you may have misunderstood my actions, Train."

"Of course you do. Otherwise, how could you live with yourself?"

"You don't want to do this to me."

"Do you remember my father's funeral? You drove me home from the cemetery."

"Kevin was a good man."

"He was an asshole." Lionel sniffles and sips the vodka. His eyes water, and he knows he could cry, but there'll be time for that later. "You bought me an ice-cream cone, pistachio with jimmies, and drove slowly. You said, 'I know for a young boy like you, Train, this is an awful loss.' By then you were patting my leg. You left your hand on my thigh . . ."

Father Tom unbuttons his coat and takes off his cap, pats down his thin, flyaway hair. He feels his forehead. He remembers those mornings in church when Jesus would come to him with His heart burning like a furnace, and the heat would blanket Tom, and he would sweat and lift his eyes to heaven, and Jesus would thrust a golden dart through his heart.

". . . and then your hand was in your pants, and your face was all squinched up, and all I could do was stare out the window and hope it would end, and the ice cream melted and ran down my arm until it was all gone."

"That did not happen, and I don't know why you want to think it did. I was offering you comfort and solace. I knew what it felt like to hunger for human touch. My father never held me, Train. Ever. My mother never did after Gerard died."

"Should I play my little violin?"

"I took your father's place."

"I'd wake up and you'd be in my bed."

"*On* your bed. Watching you sleep, like fathers have always watched their sons and imagined brilliant futures for them."

"That's fucked up."

"You were an affectionate boy. You brought out the tenderness in people. In me. And yes, I felt needed; I felt connected to another person for the first time since Gerard died."

"Did you wonder how *I* felt?"

"If it was a problem for you, you should have told me. I would have respected that. I had an understanding with myself. I thought I had your permission."

"If nothing sexual ever happened, why do I remember that it did?"

"Could you be making it up, Train?"

And then there's a knock, and Mr. Markey opens the door and steps into the room. He stamps his feet, tosses a fifth of brandy to Lionel and a newspaper to Father Tom. "You're famous, Father."

The man behind Mr. Markey takes off his glasses and his balaclava. He wipes his glasses with a hanky and puts them back on.

Mr. Markey says, "I believe you've already met my friend, Mr. Hanratty."

"Twice," Father Tom replies.

Mr. Markey says, "You'll excuse us, gents," and Lionel gets up and follows Mr. Hanratty down the hall to the kitchen.

"He's a reporter," Father Tom says.

Mr. Markey smiles. "Terrance doesn't write for the *Globe*; he delivers it."

Father Tom points to his face. "He did this to me."

"He can be a little feisty. I try to keep him on a short leash." Mr. Markey shrugs. "So tell me, Father, does our Lionel still make your heart beat faster?"

Father Tom stands and steps toward the door. "I'm not going to sit here and listen to this."

Mr. Markey grabs Father Tom's arm at the wrist and twists it until the palm is behind his back and the elbow is locked.

"I've read somewhere that pain elevates our thoughts," Mr. Markey says, and he tugs at the arm until Father Tom feels like it'll snap at the wrist and shatter at the shoulder. "Of course, I'm not a theologian."

Father Tom is bent at the waist and in tears. "Please, you're hurting me."

"Keeps our mind off amusements."

"You're insane."

"Have you ever slept on a bed of crushed glass, Father?"

"Please, dear God!"

"Worn a crown of nettle?" Mr. Markey lifts the arm slowly. "These are not rhetorical questions, Father. Answer me."

"No, I haven't."

Mr. Markey releases Father Tom and shoves him back onto the sofa. "What excruciating bliss when the pain ends. You feel grateful to me right now, don't you?"

Father Tom can't move his arm.

"Thank me."

"Thank *you?*"

Mr. Markey leans over him. "Thank me!"

"Thank you."

"You're welcome." Mr. Markey tousles Father Tom's hair, pats his head. "Pain releases endorphins. You feel a little high. I believe you have practiced certain endorphin-releasing austerities yourself, have you not?"

"I'm not a masochist, if that's what you mean."

"The time you slammed your hand in the car door?"

"An accident."

"That's not what you told your therapist. Why on earth would you have wanted to punish yourself like that?" Mr. Markey walks to the window and admires the storm. "You don't get to see but one or two nor'easters like this in a lifetime."

Father Tom wonders if he could make it out the door before Mr. Markey catches him. And then what?

"I'm sure you struggled, Father, fought the good fight. You always wanted to do the right thing, but those little cock teasers wouldn't let you. Always with their sweet little asses and their angelic smiles." He leans forward and whispers: "You liked bending their heads back and kissing their exposed throats, didn't you? Absolutely divine, isn't it?"

"You filthy—"

"An ecstatic moment and yet so difficult to put into words." Mr. Markey takes off his gloves and pulls up the sleeves of his car coat. "Nothing up my sleeve." And then he reaches behind Father Tom's ear and holds up a folded piece of loose-leaf paper. "What have we here?" He unfolds it. "My associate, Mr. Hanratty, discovered this in your dresser beneath your unmentionables while we were speaking earlier. It seems to be a list of boys' names. Should I read them?"

"Boys from the parish, boys I've worked with."

"But not *all* the boys you've worked with. What's special about these boys?"

"Everyone has his favorites."

Mr. Hanratty returns and hands a manila folder to Mr. Markey, who holds it up for Father Tom to see. "You can guess what this is, I'm sure."

"Class photos," Father Tom says.

"Of boys."

"Perfectly innocent," Father Tom says.

"They help you get off, I'll bet."

Father Tom feels the throbbing pain in his closed eye. "Look," he says, "it was a constant battle. I was always thinking about this . . . this abomination and trying not to think about it. I had no time for friendship or music or dreams or joy or charity or anything else that makes life worth living. If I had relaxed for a moment, I knew I might lose control. But I did not!"

"You are a victim of yourself. Is that what you're saying? *You're* the victim?"

Father Tom notices that the Pope's painted eyes seem to shimmer in their sockets and spin like pinwheels and Mr. Markey's voice sounds tinny and far away, and then Lionel's a boy again, and he and Lionel are kneeling by the kid's bed saying their prayers, and then he tickles Lionel until he begs him to stop, and Father Tom stops and says, *What a great relief when the pleasure ends*. And he drapes his arm around Lionel's shoulders and kisses his blond head, like a father saying good-night to his beloved son, and then, he can't help it, he tickles Lionel again until the boy yells, *Help!* And then Father Tom feels his head snap and realizes he's been slapped.

"Thanks, you needed that," Mr. Hanratty says.

"Why were you screaming for help, Father?" Mr. Markey puts the watch cap on Father Tom's head. "Let's go for a walk."

Mr. Markey closes the door behind them. He stands on the porch with Father Tom while Mr. Hanratty shovels a path through the waist-high drift to the middle of the windswept street where the snow is only shin- and ankle-deep.

"Where's Lionel?" Father Tom asks.

"Sleeping it off."

Father Tom pulls the cap down over his ears. The ringing in the left is worse. "What's the best I can hope for?"

"That we've been wrong all along, and there's no after-life."

"That's absurd."

"That way you won't know you're dead. And in hell."

"You have no right to judge me."

"Who would want to live forever anyway? We'd be so bored we'd kill ourselves."

Mr. Markey leads Father Tom to the street. Mr. Hanratty spears his shovel into the snow. All Father Tom can see out of his squinted eyes are the slanting sheets of blowing flakes, the snowy hummocks of buried cars, and the indistinct façades of houses. He hears what might be the distant drone of heavy machinery or the blood coursing through his head. Mr. Markey and Mr. Hanratty stand to either side of him and lock their arms in his. Heads bowed into the wind, they begin their trudge down I Street.

"Where are you taking me?"

Mr. Markey says, "We thought you might need help."

"I *have* hope." Hope is the last emotion to leave us, Father Tom thinks. He sees the lyre player on her rock and speculates that you don't hope *for* something, do you? You just hope. To wait is to hope. Hope is a rebuke to the cold and starless sky. *I am*, it says. *I will be.* Father Tom sees movement to his right and makes out a bundled and hooded figure sweeping snow from a porch.

Mr. Markey leans his face to Father Tom's ear and says, "Not *hope! Help!*" The figure on the porch stops, regards the three lumbering gentlemen, turns, and goes into the house. And then Mr. Markey adds, "Sometimes a message must be sent," but what Father Tom hears is "Sometimes a messy, musky scent," and he wonders why this man is speaking in riddles. Mr. Markey tells Mr. Hanratty how we all have our burden to carry, and he points to Father Tom and says, "And this is the cross-eyed bear." Why would they call him that? Father Tom wonders.

When they reach Gleason's Market, Father Tom knows the rectory is around the block, and he's relieved to see that they're taking him back. They had him rattled earlier with that talk of no afterlife and all. But what else could they do, really? Soon he'll be sipping Mrs. Walsh's potato and barley soup after a hot bath, and then he'll go to his room and read and look out on this magnificent storm. Maybe he'll read right through his Graham Greene novels like he did the winter he was laid up with the broken leg. He sees a light on in the rectory kitchen, or at least he thinks he does. With all this bone-white snow in the air, it's not like you can actually look *at* anything. You look *through* the white. It's like peering at the world through linen. But then the light goes off, or was never on, and he thinks of the tricks your eyes can pull on you, like when you stare at the sky and the clouds seem to race up and away from you. No, the light is still on. He turns to Mr. Markey and says, "Everything's all right then?"

"Copacetic, Father." Mr. Markey looks at Father Tom's florid and swollen face, at his tiny blue eye, fixed in baggy lids like a turquoise bead on a leather pouch. A ragged little thin-lipped cyclops.

They walk past the rectory and follow a path that Mr. O'Toole has evidently plowed between the garage and the school. Father Tom looks up at the fourth-grade classroom and sees his nine-year-old self in the window by the pencil sharpener, nose pressed against the glass, looking down at him. When he peers out the window, Tom sees a battered old drunk being helped home by two friends, and he would like to know whose grandfather this is, but Sister calls him back to his seat for the spelling bee. Father Tom thinks now that he remembers that stormy morning when this ungainly procession passed below the window as he watched, but the old man could not have been him. A person can't be in two places at the same time. And then Monsignor McDermott is standing in the window. Father Tom would like to wave hello, but the men have his arms. The monsignor blows his nose and wipes it and then tucks his hanky up the sleeve of his cassock. Father Tom struggles to free the arm, and his escorts release him. He waves, but to an empty window. He considers screaming but doubts his voice would carry in the muffled stillness of the snow. And if it did? He lifts his arms, and the gentlemen lock theirs in his and walk.

"That's better," Mr. Markey says.

When they head up an alley and away from the rectory, Father Tom asks Mr. Markey, "Who do you think you are?"

"Nobody."

"You're somebody."

"Am I?"

"And I think I know you."

Father Tom is warm under this snowy blanket and would like to take off his jacket. He feels the icy snow whipping at his face and sees a pearl-handled straight razor lying on a bloom of crimson snow by his groin. He's on his back. His legs are buried beneath the drift. How long has he lain here? He gurgles, coughs, tastes blood in his mouth. He'd been dreaming of falling through a starless purple sky away from the vision of Christ when he realized he was tumbling toward the infernal abyss, and he screamed himself awake, thank God. His left arm is bent at the elbow and points to heaven. He tells the arm to move, but nothing happens. He might as well be telling someone else's arm to move. He remembers long ago lying helplessly in Lionel's bed with the dozing boy and trying to will him to turn, to rest his head on his, Father Tom's, chest and his slender arm on Father's waist. And later when Lionel whimpered and opened his teary eyes, Father Tom held him and said, "You've had a bad dream, Train, that's all. Don't cry, baby, don't cry. Don't cry."

But if he did not, in fact, scream himself awake moments ago, and if this is, indeed, hell, this frozen drift of blood and guilt, then Father Tom is happy to know that at least they don't take your memories away, which makes sense, because without a past you don't exist, and there can be no hell for you. He knows that his memories of love and affection will comfort and sustain him for eternity. And then he sees Mr. Markey and Mr. Hanratty standing over him. But when Mr. Hanratty pulls back his balaclava, Father Tom sees that it's Gerard, and he's with Jesus and not with Mr. Markey, and Jesus has His arm draped over Gerard's shoulders. Jesus waves at Father Tom and says, "So long, small fry!" They shake their heads and turn away.

"Stop, please!" Father Tom says, or thinks he says. And then he watches them somehow as they walk back in the direction of St. Cormac's, watches Jesus whisper into Gerard's ear, and the two of them turn again to glance back at him, but all they see is a black smudge in a white world that looks otherwise unsullied.

PART III

VEILS OF DECEIT

THE ORIENTAL HAIR POETS

BY DON LEE

Cambridge

This was her, he figured. The poet. That was the first thing Marcella Ahn had said on the phone, that she was a poet. She was, in fact, the über-image of a poet, straight black hair hanging to her lower back, midnight-blue velvet pants, lace-up black boots, flouncy white Victorian blouse cinched by a thick leather belt. She was pretty in a severe way, too much makeup, lots of foundation and powder, deep claret lipstick, early thirties, maybe. Not his type. She stumbled through Café Pamplona's small door and, spotting Toua, clomped to his table.

"Am I late? Sorry. I'm not quite awake. It's a little early in the day for me." It was 1:30 in the afternoon.

She ordered a double espresso and gathered her hair, the ruffled cuffs of her blouse dropping away, followed by the jangling cascade of two dozen silver bracelets on each wrist. With exquisitely lacquered fingers, silver rings on nearly every digit, she raked her hair over her shoulder and laid it over her left breast.

"Don't you have an office? It feels a little exposed in here for this type of conversation."

Actually, this was precisely why Toua Xiong liked the café. The Pamplona was a tiny basement place off Harvard Square, made to feel even smaller with its low ceiling, and you could hear every tick of conversation from across the room. Perfect for initial meetings with clients. It forced them to lean toward him, huddle, whisper. It didn't lend itself to histrionics or hysterics. It inhibited weeping. Toua didn't like weeping.

Besides, he no longer had an office. After Ana, his girlfriend, had kicked him out of their apartment, he'd been sleeping in his office, but he'd gotten behind on the rent and had been kicked out of there too. These days he was sacking out on his former AA sponsor's couch.

"You used to be a cop, Mr. Xiong?" she asked, pronouncing it *Zee-ong*.

"Yeah," he said, "until two years ago."

"You still have friends on the force?"

"A few."

"Why'd you quit?"

"Complicated," Toua said. "*Shee-ong*. It's *Too-a Shee-ong*."

"Chinese?"

"Hmong."

"I'm Korean myself."

"What is it I can do for you, Ms. Ahn?"

She straightened up in her chair. "I have a tenant," she said in a clear, unrestrained voice, not at all inhibited. "She's renting one of my houses in Cambridgeport, and she's on a campaign to destroy me."

Toua nodded, accustomed to hyperbole from clients. "What's she doing?"

"She's trying to drive me insane. I asked her to move out. I gave her thirty days' notice. But she's refused."

"You have a lease?"

"She's a tenant at will."

"Shouldn't be too difficult to evict her, then."

"You know how hard it is to evict someone in Cambridge? Talk about progressive laws."

"It sounds like you need a lawyer, not a PI."

"You don't understand. Recently, she started sending me anonymous *gifts*. Like candy and flowers, then things like stuffed animals and scarves and hairbrushes and, you know, barrettes—almost like she has a *crush* on me. Then it got even creepier. She sent me *lingerie*."

"How do you know it was her? Maybe you have a secret admirer."

"Please. I have a lot of admirers, but she's not one of them. I know it was her."

"Well, the problem is, none of that's against the law, or even considered threatening."

"Exactly! You see how conniving she is? She's diabolical!"

"Uh-huh." He took a sip of his coffee. "Why do you think she's doing these things?"

"I don't know. I've been nothing but charitable toward her."

"Although there was that minor thing of asking her to move out."

"Look, something really strange has been happening. I got a high-meter-read warning from the Water Department. The bill last month was $2,500. You know what that amounts to? She's been using almost ten thousand gallons of water a *day*." She dug into her purse and produced the statement.

"*This* is grounds for eviction," Toua said, looking at it. "Excessive water use."

"That's what I thought. But it's not that simple. It could be contested as a faulty meter or leak or something, even though I've had all that checked out. She categorically denies anything's amiss. You see what I mean? She's trying to play with my *mind*. What I need is evidence. I need proof of what she's *doing* in there."

Ten thousand gallons a day. Toua couldn't imagine. The woman had to be running open every faucet, shower, and spigot in the house 24/7, punching on the dish and clothes washers over and over, flushing the toilets ad nauseum. Or maybe experimenting with some indoor hydroponic farming, growing ganja.

"I guess I could do a little surveillance," he said, giving the water bill back to Marcella Ahn.

"Round the clock?"

Toua laughed. "I have other cases. I have a life," he said, though neither was true.

"I own another house on the same lot, a studio. The tenant just left. You could move in there for the duration."

"You realize what this might cost?" he asked, trying to decide how much he could squeeze out of Marcella Ahn.

"That's not an issue for me," she said. "I want to know everything. I want to know every little thing she's been doing or is planning to do, what she's saying about the situation and me to other people, what's going on in her life, a full profile. The more I know, the more I can protect myself. Your ad said something about computer forensics?" Business had gotten so bad, Toua had been reduced to stuffing promotional fliers into mailboxes, targeting the wealthy demographic along Brattle Street, where people could afford to act on their suspicions, infidelity being the most common. "Can you hack into her e-mail?"

"I won't do anything illegal," he told her.

"You won't, or can't?"

"Anything I get trespassing would be inadmissible in court."

"Would it be trespassing if I gave you a key?"

"That's a gray area."

"As are so many things in this world, Mr. *Shee-ong.* I don't care what it takes. Do whatever you have to do. I want this woman out of my life."

Marcella Ahn, it turned out, was something of a slumlady. The house in Cambridgeport was a mess, a two-bedroom cape with rotting clapboards, rusted-out chain link, the yard overflowing with weeds and detritus. The second house was a converted detached garage in back, equally decrepit. Toua spent two days cleaning it, bringing an inflatable bed and some furnishings from his storage unit to try to make it habitable.

The studio did, however, provide a good vantage point for surveillance. The driveway and side door were directly in front of him, and a couple of large windows at the back of the main house gave Toua a view into the kitchen through to the living room. He set up his video camera and watched the tenant.

Caroline Yip was an Asian waif, five-two, barely a hundred pounds. Like Marcella Ahn, she had spectacular butt-length hair, but it was wavy, seldom brushed, by the looks of it. She had none of Marcella Ahn's artifices, wearing ragtag, threadbare clothes—flip-flops, holes in her T-shirts and jeans—and no makeup whatsoever. She was athletic, jogging every morning, doing yoga in the afternoons, and using a clunky old bike for transportation; her movements were quick, decisive, careless. She chucked things about, her mail, the newspaper, dishes, flatware, never giving anything a second glance. Her internal engine was jittery, in constant need of locomotion and replenishment. Despite her tiny size, she ate like a hog, slurping up bowls of cereal and crunching down on toast with peanut butter throughout the day, fixing mammoth sandwiches for lunch, and stir-frying whole heads of bok choy with chicken, served on mounds of rice, for dinner.

During one of those first nights, after Caroline Yip had left on her bicycle, Toua entered the house. From what he had observed, he was not expecting tidiness, but he was still taken aback by the interior's condition. The woman was an immense slob. Her only furnishings were a couch and a coffee table (obviously street finds), a boom box, a futon, and a few ugly lamps, the floors littered with clothes, CDs, shoes, books, papers, and magazines. There was a thick layer of grease on the stove and countertops, dust and hair and curdled food on every other surface, and the bathroom was clogged with sixty-two bottles of shampoo and conditioner, some half-filled, most of them empty. No photos or posters adorned the walls, no decorations anywhere, and there were no extra place settings for guests. She didn't need companionship, it appeared, didn't need mementos of her family or her past, reminders of her origins or her identity. She was a transient. Her house was a functional dump. Her attention resided elsewhere.

By poking through her bills, pay stubs, calendar, and checkbook, Toua gleaned several more things: Caroline Yip had no money and lousy credit; she taught classes at three different colleges as a poorly paid adjunct instructor; she supported herself mainly by waitressing at Chez Henri four nights a week; she had no appointments whatsoever, not with a lover or friend or family member or even a dentist, in the foreseeable future.

He downloaded her e-mail and website usernames and passwords and configured her wireless modem so he could access her laptop covertly, but there wasn't much activity there, nothing unusual. Nor did her cell phone calls, which he was able to pick up on his radio scanner, merit much interest over the next few days, nothing more personal than scheduling shifts at work. She was a loner. She didn't have a life. Just like him.

She was also, like Toua, an insomniac. On consecutive nights, he saw her bedroom light snapping on for a while, going out, turning on, which explained the dark circles under her eyes and the strange ritual she practiced in the mornings, meditating on the living room floor, beginning the sessions by trying to relax her face, stretching and contorting it, mouth yowling open, eyes bulging—a horrific sight. What kept her up at night? What was worrying Caroline Yip, preoccupying her?

She would end up supplying the answers herself. He supposed, given their proximity, that it was inevitable they would run into each other. The morning of his fifth day, as he was walking down the driveway, she surprised him by coming out the side door, laundry basket in hand. He thought she'd left on her jog already.

"Oh, hey," she said. "You're my new neighbor, aren't you?"

They introduced themselves, shaking hands.

"Where'd you live before this?" she asked.

"Agassiz," he said. "You know, near Dali."

"I love that restaurant."

"How about you? How long you been here?"

"Oh, four years or so."

Up close, she was more appealing than he'd anticipated. As opposed to Marcella Ahn, she was exactly his type, natural, unpretentious, a little shy, forgetful but not at all ditzy, not unlike his ex-girlfriend. Toua had to remind himself that Caroline Yip was the subject of his investigation, and that she was, in all probability, unstable, if not out-and-out dangerous.

"Hey, I gotta go," she said, "but if you're not doing anything later, we can have a drink in the garden." They both looked over at the "garden," broken concrete slabs and crab-grass where a battered wire table and two cracked plastic chairs were perched, and they shared a smirk. "I make a mean gin and tonic."

"I don't drink," he told her.

"Iced tea, then."

It was a bit unorthodox, but Toua accepted the invitation. He thought it'd give him an opportunity to probe, so he met her outside at 6, Caroline Yip bringing out two tall glasses of iced tea, Toua a plate of cheese and crackers.

They made small talk, mostly chatting about the neighborhood, the laundromat, nearby stores, takeout places—soul food from the Coast Café on River Street, steak tips from the Village Grill on Magazine. Then, as casually as he could, Toua asked, "What's the owner of this property like?"

"What do you mean?"

"She a decent landlord? She fix things when they break?"

"She's a cunt."

"Okay," he said. He had thought he'd have to work a little harder to uncover her feelings. He had agreed to give Marcella Ahn daily e-mail updates, but thus far he'd had nothing to report. Caroline Yip wasn't doing anything untoward in the house, and her water usage, according to the meter, which he dutifully checked every day, was normal. He had begun to think this was all a figment of Marcella Ahn's imagination, that the gifts had been from a fan (did poets have fans?), that the meter had been malfunctioning or there'd indeed been a leak. But now, startled by the vehemence with which Caroline Yip said "cunt," he reconsidered. "Why do you say that?"

"Let's talk about something else. Want a refill?"

She took their glasses and went into the kitchen. She returned with a gin and tonic for herself.

"When'd you quit drinking?" she asked, handing him his iced tea.

"The first time?" Toua said. "After college."

"There must be a story there."

"Long story. I'll tell it to you some other time, maybe."

"I'm interested."

"It's not very interesting."

"Come on. Start at the beginning. Where'd you grow up?"

She kept pressing, and finally he told her the story, not bothering to disguise it. When he was three, his family had fled Laos to the Ban Vinai refugee camp in Thailand, where they spent three years before being shipped off to White Bear, Minnesota. He worked hard in school and was accepted to M.I.T., but once there he felt overwhelmed, afraid he couldn't cut it, and he started drinking. In his sophomore year, he flunked out. He enlisted in the army and served as an MP in Kuwait during the first Gulf War, then returned to the States and joined the Cambridge Police, going to night school at Suffolk for years and finally getting his degree. Eventually he made detective, staying sober until two years ago, after which he quit the force.

"What happened?" she asked.

"It wasn't one thing. It was everything. I burned out." He was working on a new task force. A gang called MOD, Methods of Destruction, made up of Hmong teenagers, had moved into Area 4, and Toua was given the assignment because everyone assumed he spoke Hmong. Drive-bys, home invasions, extortion, drugs, firearms, prostitution—MOD was into it all, even sending notices to cops that they'd been "green-lighted" for execution. Toua received one, emblazoned with MOD's slogan, *Cant Stop, Wont Stop*. But the real menace was to victims picked at random. A couple coming out of a restaurant

was robbed and macheted to death. A college coed was kid-
napped and gang-raped for days. A family was tied up and
tortured with pliers and a car battery, their baby scalded with
boiling water. Senseless. Toua didn't want to see it anymore.

"Jesus. Are these guys still around?"

"Some. I heard most of them have moved on."

"I had no idea. I've always thought Cambridge was so safe.
What have you been doing since?"

"Not a lot," Toua said. He had revealed too much. He
didn't know why. Perhaps because he hadn't talked to anyone
in quite a while. "What about you? What do you do?"

"I'm a poet," she told him.

He was an idiot. A lazy idiot. He had taken the client's word
for granted, when a simple Google search would have revealed
the truth.

"You lied to me," Toua said to Marcella Ahn at her
house.

"Lying is a relative term," she replied, once again decked out
as an Edwardian whore: a corset and bodice, miniskirt and high
heels, full makeup, hair glistening. "I might have omitted a few
things. Maybe it was a test, to see how competent you are."

"She has every reason to hate you."

"Oh? Is that what she told you? I'm the one at fault for her
being such a failure?"

For several years, the two women had been the best of
friends—inseparable, really. But then their first books came
out at the same time, Marcella Ahn's from a major New York
publisher, Caroline Yip's from a small, albeit respected press.
Both had very similar jacket photos, the two women looking
solemn and precious, hair flowing in full regalia. An unfortunate coincidence. Critics couldn't resist reviewing them to-

gether, mocking the pair as "The Oriental Hair Poets," "The Braids of the East," and "The New Asian Poetresses."

But Marcella Ahn came away from these barbs relatively unscathed. Her book, *Speak to Desire*, was taken seriously, compared to Marianne Moore and Emily Dickinson. Her poetry was highly erudite, usually beginning with mundane observations about birds or plant life, then slipping into long, abstract meditations on entropy and inertia, the Bible, evolution, and death, punctuated by the briefest mention of personal deprivations—anorexia, depression, abandonment. Or so the critics said. Toua couldn't make heads or tails of the poems he found online.

In contrast, Caroline Yip's book, *Chicks of Chinese Descent*, was skewered. She wrote in a slangy, contemporary voice, full of topical pop culture allusions. She wrote about masturbation and Marilyn Monroe, about tampons and moo goo gai pan, about alien babies and chickens possessed by the devil. She was roundly dispatched as a mediocre talent.

Worse, in Caroline Yip's eyes, was what happened afterward. She accused Marcella of trying to thwart her at every turn. Teaching jobs, coveted magazine publications, awards, residencies, fellowships—everything Caroline applied for, Marcella seemed to get. Caroline told people it didn't hurt that Marcella was a shameless schmoozer, flirting and networking with anyone who might be of use. Yet the fact was, Marcella was rich. Her father was a shipping tycoon, and she had a trust fund in the millions. She didn't need any of these pitifully small sinecures which would have meant a livelihood to Caroline, and she came to believe that the only reason Marcella was pursuing them at all was to taunt her.

"You see now why she's doing these things?" Marcella Ahn said. "I've let her stay in that house practically rent-free, and how does she repay me? By smearing me. Spreading anonymous rumors on Internet forums! Implying I slept with award judges! Posting bad reviews of my book! So enough was enough. I stopped speaking to her and asked her to move out. Was that unreasonable of me? After all I've done for her? I lent her money. I kept encouraging her. I helped her find a publisher for her book. What did I get in return? A hateful squatter who's trying to mindfuck me, who's intent on the destruction of my reputation and sanity!"

This was, Toua thought to himself, silly. He glanced around Marcella Ahn's plush, immaculate house. Mahogany floor, custom wood furniture. Didn't these women have anything better to do than engage in petty games? And what did this say about him? He'd given up his shield only to go from trailing husbands to skip-tracing debtors and serving subpoenas to accommodating the paranoid whims of two crackpot poets.

"I think I should quit," he said.

"Quit?" Marcella Ahn snapped. "You can't quit. Not *now*. I think she's preparing to do something. I think she's planning to *harm* me."

"She's not doing anything. You've gotten my reports."

"Maybe she suspects. Maybe she's stopped because she thinks she's being watched."

"I seriously doubt it."

"Why won't you believe me?" Marcella Ahn asked. "Why?" And then she began to weep.

"Is it too late?"

"No, I was awake."

"You sound tired."

"Long day. I drove down to see Mom."

"How's she doing?"

"Better, I guess. Still kind of frail."

"What else you been up to?"

"The usual. Work. You?"

"Nothing too exciting."

"You know you can't keep calling like this."

"Is he there?"

"Not the point."

"Is he?"

"No."

"How is Pritchett?"

"Stop."

"Ana, I still love you."

"I know."

"You know? That's it? You know?"

"I don't want to keep doing this. It's painful."

"Let me see: you cheat on me, with Pritchett of all people, you kick me out, and you're the one in pain."

"Have you been drinking?"

"No."

"What do you want me to say?"

"Say . . . say there's a chance."

"There's not. Not right now, there's not."

"But maybe things will change?"

"Don't do this to yourself."

"This is all I have, Ana. This is all I have."

He watched her. He monitored her e-mail. He listened to her calls. He logged the numbers from the water meter every day. He talked to her, once more sat in the garden with her.

He had let Marcella Ahn persuade him to stay on, particularly after, as an additional incentive, she had offered him more money. Yet increasingly he felt it was a pointless exercise. He was convinced more than ever that Caroline Yip was oblivious to any of the transgressions of which she was being accused, oblivious to the fact that Toua was working for Marcella Ahn or even knew of their past. He was bored. At the end of the week, he would quit for good. By then he'd have the security deposit for an apartment.

Thursday night, Caroline Yip knocked on his door. "I'm going to the Cantab. Wanna come?"

The Cantab Lounge was a dive bar in Central Square, known for its music and cheap drinks. The last time he fell off the wagon, Toua had been a regular there. He'd bar-hop down Mass. Ave., beginning with the Cellar, then moving on to the Plough & Stars and the People's Republik, ending the night at the Cantab, each place seedier than the last.

It was early still at the Cantab, the first set yet to begin, and they decided to first go across the street to Picante for a bite. They ordered chicken tostadas with a steak quesadilla to share, and they sat at a table beside the front window after loading up on salsa.

"How're your poems going?" he asked.

"*Así así.*"

"What?"

"So-so," she said. "Find a job yet?"

"Not yet."

"I imagine it'd be easy for you to do something in security. What about private investigator work?"

Was she being coy? "I'll look into it."

"I have a question for you," Caroline said. She wiped guacamole from the corner of her mouth. "What is it that you fear the most?"

"Like phobias?"

"No, about yourself. About your life. How you'll end up."

It was an awful question, one that immediately dropped him into a funk. And although he didn't realize he had been ruminating on it, he knew the answer right away. "Dead man walking," he said.

"What? As in being led down death row?" She laughed nervously. "Feeling homicidal these days?"

He shook his head. He told her about the look he'd seen in some perps, the MOD gangbangers in particular, the vacancy in their eyes, a complete lacuna, devoid of any hope or humanity. "I'm afraid I might become like that. Dead. Soulless."

"The fact that it worries you insures you won't."

"I don't know."

Caroline took a big bite of the quesadilla, chewed, swallowed. "I fear that all the sacrifices I've made for my poetry will have been for nothing, that really I have no talent, that someday I'll realize this but won't be able to admit it, because to do so would invalidate my life, so instead I'll become resentful of anyone who's had the slightest bit of success, lash out at them with stupid, spiteful acts of malice, rail against an unfair system and world and fate that's denied me my rightful place of honor and glory. I'll become a cold, bitter person. I'll never find peace, or love, or purpose. I'll die alone."

He nodded. "I'm glad you brought this up. I'm feeling really good now. Very cheerful."

Caroline giggled. "Let's go listen to some music."

The Cantab was in full swing now, and Toua and Caroline squeezed through the crowd to the bar. "Yo, Toua-Boua, long time no see," boomed Large Marge, one of the bartenders. "What's your pleasure?"

He got a rum and Coke for Caroline, a plain Coke for himself. Miraculously, they found a couple of chairs against the far wall, and they listened to the R&B band on the stage. The place hadn't changed a bit, the green walls, the faux-Tiffany lamps with the Michelob Light logos, the net of Christmas lights on the ceiling, the usual barflies and post-hippy gray-beards in the audience.

Sitting there, it did occur to Toua that Caroline had impli-cated herself, expressing exactly the vindictive mindset that Marcella Ahn had described. What did it matter, though? What did it matter? It was all so trivial.

When he went to the bar for another round, he ordered two rum and Cokes. It tasted like crap—Jameson, neat, with a chaser of Guinness had been his poison of choice—but since Caroline was drinking it, she wouldn't be able to smell the alcohol on his breath.

After several more rum and Cokes, Caroline hauled him onto the dance floor, and they swayed and bumped against each other, jostled by the sweating couples around them.

Caroline hooked her arms around his neck. "I like you," she shouted.

"I like you too," he said, and they kissed.

It was so good to feel something, he thought. To feel any-thing.

They woke up together the next morning on Caroline's futon. "Was this a mistake?" she asked.

"Probably."

"You weren't supposed to say that."

She made him breakfast—cereal, scrambled eggs, coffee, toast with peanut butter. "Do you ever think of leaving Cam-bridge?"

"To go where?" he asked.

"California. I went through a little town south of San Francisco once, Rosarita Bay. It's a sleepy little place, very quiet. It's not very pretty or anything, but for some reason it draws me. I love the idea of making a fresh start there, no one knowing who I am."

"Sounds nice." His head was pounding; he could have used a drink.

"Not tempted to join me someday?" she said hesitantly. He must have appeared alarmed, because she laughed and got a little defensive. "That was impulsive. Stupid. Never mind."

"Not stupid. Just sudden."

"Too sudden?"

He looked at Caroline. He did not know this woman. He was not in love with her, and she was not in love with him. But they might grow to love each other. It was possible. It seemed like the first opening of possibility in his life in a very long time, a fissure. "Maybe not."

She had to go to Chez Henri soon. She was pulling a double shift, covering for another waitress. "We'll talk more tomorrow?"

"We'll talk more tomorrow," he told her.

He was awoken before dawn. He had gone to bed early and fell dead asleep—the first good night's sleep he'd had in months, hangover-induced, no doubt. On the other end of the phone was Pritchett. "Want to come down here?"

"Here" was Marcella Ahn's house. When Toua drove up to it, a fire truck, an ambulance, two black-and-whites, and an unmarked police car were parked out front.

"What's going on?" he asked Pritchett, his former partner.

The inside of the house had been trashed, furniture overturned and broken, upholstery shredded, wine bottles smashed onto the floors and splattered on the rugs, paintings tattered, clothes scissored into strips, mirrors shattered. *Can't Stop. Won't Stop* was spray-painted on one wall, *Cunt* on the front door.

"Anything taken?" Toua asked.

"Strange, not much," Pritchett said, "just a laptop and some notebooks and fountain pens. We found them down the street in a dumpster. Notice anything else out of whack?"

"Yeah."

Marcella Ahn was in the ambulance, a blanket over her shoulders, shaking and crying. She had been out of town for a reading, returning to find her house in ruins. "Do you believe me now?" she said to Toua. "Do you believe me now? It's *her.* I'm *sure* of it."

"What's this all about?" Pritchett asked him.

He had been a fool. He had trusted her, had let himself get lulled into careless affection for her.

Based on Toua's statement and case reports, they arrested Caroline Yip, and, knowing that with no record she'd make bail, they issued a restraining order against her.

It had been a decent ruse, and it might have worked, everyone believing the MOD were on another search-and-rampage mission but had been spooked by something—a noise, a neighbor—into leaving before they could gut the house of its possessions, except for one small but critical error. *Can't Stop. Won't Stop*, besides being unusually well-punctuated with apostrophes and a period, had been sprayed with blue paint. The MOD were Bloods—red bandanna. Blue was the color of the Crips, their rivals.

In the end, the charges against Caroline were dropped. She had no alibi for the hours after the restaurant closed at 10:30, but there was little evidence to prosecute her, no prints, no eyewitnesses of a woman with long hair on a bicycle, nothing incriminating found in her house like a spray-paint can or soiled clothes.

Nonetheless, Caroline Yip chose to leave town. Toua saw her as she was packing up a U-Haul van to drive to California.

"She used you, you know."

"I think if anyone did, *you* used me," Toua said.

"You have a funny way of interpreting things. Don't you get it? She faked it. She set me up. Set *you* up. Hasn't that occurred to you? Marcella invented this insidious plot to frame me and run me out of town."

"Why would she do that?"

"Who knows. What makes one person want to destroy another? Huh? She has everything, yet it's not enough."

"There's no point in pretending anymore."

"She's a vulture. She has some sick bond to me. She *needs* to humiliate me. She *needs* my misery. She can't function without it."

"You need help."

She slammed the doors to the van shut. "I feel sorry for you," Caroline said. "You missed it. It could have been something real, and you missed it."

He watched her maneuver the van down the driveway and onto the street, then headed inside the studio to pack his own possessions. He had things to do. First on the list, he needed a bed for his new apartment.

Could Marcella Ahn have been that smart and calculating? He hadn't looked at the water bill very closely. She could have doctored it. She could have known all along that he'd been on the MOD task force. She could have wrecked her own home, orchestrating everything to this outcome.

He picked up his duffel bag. He didn't want to believe it.

Believing it would mean that Caroline was right, he'd missed his chance to emerge from the deadness he felt. It was easier to believe, all things considered, that he'd been betrayed by her. She was a devious person, a liar, conniving and malicious, rent with envy, hopelessly bitter. It was comforting to think so. He could live with that kind of evil. It had a passion and direction he could understand, even a touch of poetry.

THE COLLAR

BY ITABARI NJERI

Roxbury

H ey. You better snap the fuck out if it," Nina told him, popping her fingers in a circle around his head. "She's not your friend. She's the *en-na-mee*," Nina half sang. Didn't think she had to emphasize the obvious to a thirty-two-year-old ex-Marine on his way to a doctorate from M.I.T. But the more she heard, the more she wondered about the terms of discharge and criteria for admission.

Isaac faced an assault charge that was aggravated, Nina discovered, by stupidity: violation of a restraining order.

"You don't know to cross the street if you see her?"

"She was boarding the same bus."

"What's your point?" That's all they had at Dudley Station, transfer point to anywhere in Boston—buses. "Take another one."

And his stab at "resolving things"—on the crowded #1 to Cambridge—happened *after* the arraignment.

At the arraignment, his best friend showed up with both sets of grandparents, a trio of uncles, and a chorus of cousins.

"I didn't know she had that many relatives in America," the ex-corporal droned, still shocked and awed.

Nina tilted her close-cropped curls and smiled, picturing it. "You think she flew some in from Johannesburg?"

"And she was wearing her collar." Isaac said it in a slow monotone matching the zombie gaze that was pissing Nina off. "I've known that girl three years and I ain't never seen her wear her collar."

The divinity school grad had a tongue-twisting South African name. Isaac called her *Sindi* for short. Nina Sojo liked *Collar*, and couldn't help smiling a little when she thought of her. Collar wanted blood.

They were sitting at Nina's dining table. A used Queen Anne repro someone had painted high-gloss white. The chairs too. Isaac drew his finger down the side of an ice-filled glass of lemonade. He examined the trail.

"Do you want me to help you find a lawyer or not?"

He winced, but kept looking at the glass.

Nina pulled back, slow and haughty. Frowning deepened the groove between her brows. It was the only line in her bare moon face. She never wore makeup offstage.

The Boston Yellow Pages was sitting there on the table. She'd been looking up lawyers. Now she stared through him, picked up the directory, and gave him her half-bare back. The crisp white top was sleeveless and gathered in a tie under her holstered breasts. The naked skin from there to her hips was the color of dark honey. The jeans gripped just below her waist. Everything looked tight. But unlike those tits, lay Nina flat, and the twins danced the slide. Shock at her body's betrayal lent Nina Isaac's zombie stare. She'd had to smack herself one morning while looking in the mirror. It is what it is, she finally told herself. The change had happened between cities and lovers. Vancouver and Boston. The economist and the chemical engineer. The engineer hadn't minded: Isaac made clear the pussy was good. "Hot and wet. Just the way I like it." But post-forty pussy stayed in the house. You didn't date it. You could take it to Starbucks, but not to see *Monster's Ball*. "You kidding?" Isaac had shook his head at the accusation. "Oh. Okay. I tell you what: let's flip the script and do the movie. Cause it's not like you really hittin' that other thang too good. Know what I'm sayin'?" She had counted on the lockdown to make him want it. When he did: "Uh-uh. You don't know how to treat me." That was February. It was June now. Pussy was still on strike.

She pushed the phone book onto a loaded shelf, then rummaged the refrigerator to make a doggie bag for Isaac's cousin Devon.

Two sets of tall bookcases standing back-to-back divided the kitchen area from the rest of the bright, loftlike unit. She'd moved in two days after 9/11. The space was a quality reno off Moreland in one of Roxbury's historic districts. Unpacked boxes draped with white sheets were still ghostly roommates after nine months. The stacked cartons formed an undulating cityscape and dividing line. On one side: her Yamaha Clavinova and shelved music collection. On the other: a computer workstation near the dining table that doubled as a desk, two halogen torch lamps, and Isaac on her futon. Staring at the ceiling lights and fake-wood trusses. Or just in that direction.

Isaac asked her something she pretended not to hear.

About now, she was feeling the Newark brother who'd put those bookshelves together. Always helpful, fun over a beer, and a professional cook who had dinner waiting when she came home. And the dick was good. Just too much insecurity attached. He never finished high school. Dropped out to raise two younger brothers who did. She thought all that admirable and said so. But Chef was always comparing himself to someone like Isaac. *Dr. M.I.T.*, the chef called him.

What came *after* was always the best part of sex with Isaac. Wet clinches in a hot shower. Long, Marine-hard body. Infinitesimal dick. Isaac was a cuddler. The curves of their bodies met in wet suction and held. Tight. In her mouth, his tongue was well-schooled. Between her thighs, his fingers were too. When she was light-headed in the steam, Isaac Sayif's tenderness could feel like love.

His hand touched her shoulder.

"Did you say you knew a judge?" he repeated.

Nina had been away from Boston for decades. But she'd known a lot of law students when she was going to Berklee. Some built major practices in the city. Some occasionally stayed in touch. Unfortunately, none were criminal attorneys.

"Maybe he could recommend someone." Isaac put his other hand on her shoulder and leaned into her back.

"Maybe *she* could," Nina responded. "But what are you going to do for money?"

He said nothing and let go of her shoulders.

"Hand me that foil, please." Nina gestured toward the refrigerator top with a paring knife. She wrapped a couple of homemade shortcakes in foil, then put a quart of strawberries she'd bought at the farmer's market that morning in a plastic bag. Two loin lamb chops left from the night's dinner went in too. Isaac had told her he liked lamb and she'd bought six on sale months ago. She offered him the bag. "For Devon."

Isaac ignored it and searched her face.

Nina didn't want to see a brother, who'd risen by straps attached to the thinnest air, get screwed. Realizing he was dazed, due in court seventy-two hours from now, and relying on the system's counsel to keep his record clean and career on track, had put her in Rescue Mama mode. But she'd just heard two hours of stupid and took off the cape.

She put her good food back in the refrigerator.

The kitchen space was cramped. Standing-room only.

Nina was a few inches shy of Isaac's five-ten. She crossed her arms and her elbow brushed his shirt front. "This woman's after your neck. Why?" Fill in the blanks, she told him. "How you better than Triple-A? You don't even own a car?"

"She knew I had Devon's ride."

"That's not his car."

"It's his car whenever he wants it," Isaac told her. Every syllable dripped smug, making Nina pause.

Sindi had called him around 3 in the morning back in March.

"She was stranded out in Newton," Isaac said.

"That time of night? How come?"

He said she'd been coming back from Wellesley.

"The college?"

He nodded. "The transmission gave out."

"And Marine to the rescue?"

"I get there and she picks a fight."

"About?"

"Bullshit."

"Yeah, that's what I say."

"I'm telling you. It was about *nuth-in*," he insisted. "She's all up in my face and I push her away. She starts swinging at me. I grab her wrists and push her back. The shit is crazy so I leave her there."

"That's it?"

"She tells the cops I assaulted her."

"You put your hands on her. That's all it takes."

He froze for a few seconds, then mumbled, "Am I that kind of man?"

Nina tried to read him. "This chick apparently sets you up and you're seriously pondering the nature of your soul?"

"She likes that," Isaac said, the drugged gaze fading.

"Likes what?"

"Being slapped around."

Nina let that hang a moment.

"She wanted me to smack her around in bed."

"Did you?"

"That is so against my spirit," he said, slowly.

Nina considered his words, his tone. Then: "What about the polygamy thing? Girlfriend down with that?" When they first met, Isaac had told Nina that he planned to move to South Africa to teach and live with multiple wives. Nina had laughed it off and said, "You must want some serious voodoo on your ass."

He shrugged now.

"That's not an answer."

"Kind of," he said.

"As long as she's Wife Number One and you beat the crap out her daily? Nig-grow, *please*." She started putting together another container of strawberries for later. She felt her sweet tooth calling.

Isaac moved toward the front door to put on his shoes.

Nina walked and talked. Fruit in one hand, paring knife in the other. "Is anything I know about you true?"

He bent to tie his shoelace. Nina hovered.

"What are you talking about?" He was holding up the wall with his shoulder and looked exhausted from the effort.

"Maybe you're that brother from another planet," 'cause she didn't know any brothers from the 'hood who talked to the police without a lawyer.

They had called him, he repeated. They'd asked if he wanted to clear things up. "I felt it could easily be resolved. This woman is my best friend. We're used to talking a dozen times a day."

"You broke up and still talked a dozen times a day?"

"Yeah."

"But she was cool with you not fucking her anymore, and you believed that?"

Nina started remembering threads of their early conversations last fall. Calling himself a free agent. Admitting, only when Nina pressed, that he did see one sister more than anyone else . . .

. . . and that Isaac had been in her car when an old boyfriend called to apologize for ancient misdeeds. It was one of those twelve-step-make-amends things. Isaac had said he thought that was nice. She'd agreed. "Especially since I stabbed him."

"She's my best friend," Isaac repeated.

Nina batted the air and a bit of forgotten strawberry flew. She needed to wash the smashed fruit off her hand. "Say goodnight, Gracie," she muttered, walking back to the kitchen.

"What?"

"Way before your time."

"Thanks for dinner," he called out from the doorway.

She ignored the lame farewell and wiped the fruit off the floor. The downstairs door slammed shut.

The night was cool and windy. Nina raised the slats of a shutter and watched Isaac disappear in the dark. It was a ten-minute walk to Dudley Station, past some very sketchy territory. Nina had escaped Boston in the '80s, the years when crack was king and a Roxbury zip code meant perpetual violence. Before the plague, she'd traveled Interstate 90 from Albany to attend Berklee, and had lived at a series of Roxbury addresses with no problem. She loved the familiar swagger and grace amidst despair. Some of those blocks had crashed and resurrected. Some meant constant crossfire still. Her new address was safe in the daytime, but a game try at night without klieg-light battalions. Nina wouldn't hazard a night stroll. But a Marine might make it.

It was past 11:00. Too late to take that second pill. The mood elevator needed to drop a few floors. Nina made a three-bag cup of Sleepytime tea and spiked it with thirty drops of valerian root. Better than Xanax and safer. She stuck a straw in the thermos mug she kept in the crib—the other stayed in the car—and popped a white noise CD in the boom box. Waves crashed. Seagulls cried. She logged on and sent an e-mail to Darcelle, the judge. Nina gave her the short of it, then wrote:

> *Don't know the "truth" of the situation, but his life story is admirable. Foster kid from the 'hood, East St. Lou*

She stopped typing, grabbed a large pink Post-it, and scribbled a note to herself: *Legal name? Isaac Elimu Sayif?* She circled it, then wrote, *AKA?* She started typing again.

> *Works at Popeyes for years, looks in the mirror, decides to wipe off the grease, joins the Marines, goes to community college, St. Louis U, then chemical engineering at M.I.T. He's all but dissertation. Plans to teach at U of Cape Town this fall. Would hate to see him derailed by B.S.*

> *Look forward to hearing from you and seeing you soon.*
> *Nina*

Nina had received a *Welcome back* message from Darcelle last month. An invitation too: the judge's annual Fourth of

July Louis Armstrong Birthday Bash. Nina had been happy to get it but surprised. She certainly hadn't announced her return to Boston. She'd worked the East Coast as a jazz singer and the world as a backup singer all through the '80s. But touring wore her out. Lost too many friends to drugs. And she'd deliberately been under the radar for a decade. Teaching mostly. Private piano lessons. Music theory and history courses at assorted colleges. She'd just finished teaching a jazz history course at Roxbury Community College. But she got the biggest rush teaching music to disabled kids in the public schools. That had brought her back to Berklee. She was studying music therapy.

She wiggled deep into the feather body pillow on the futon and settled on her side, hands in prayer position between her drawn knees. "East St. Louis," she said out loud. What part of East St. Louis don't know not to talk to a cop? A seagull cried. "That's what I'm talking about," she told the bird. "Ain't he never seen *Law & Order?*" The woman who adopted him used to be crazy with the electric cord on his ass, Isaac had told her. "She bang your head up too, baby? That the problem?"

Her phone rang before the alarm clock. She ignored both and slept past 10:00. Her body required eight or nine hours of sleep and took it. That's one reason she'd stopped touring. She washed her face, brushed her teeth, gargled with hydrogen peroxide, then popped her morning elevator. She took her ritual cup of hot lemonade with honey to the computer and found a message from the judge. Darcelle was out of town but gave Nina the name of a female attorney in Roxbury. Nina forwarded it to Isaac, then tried his cell. She ignored his voice mail and tried the house.

"Hey, Miss Nina," Devon answered before the second ring.

"Now that's how I know you love me. You screened me in. What you been up to?"

"Working, working, working."

"One would have been enough. More makes me suspicious. How's the grades?"

"I'm passing."

He was a grown hard-back man now—or thought he was. She had to tread lightly. Concern without badgering. She asked about his plans for the summer.

"I'm going to work the rest of the year and go back full-time next spring."

She feared he would never make it back. "Not many students live rent-free. Do you really need to work full-time?"

"The rent's free, but that's not exactly money in my pocket."

Nina always thought his living arrangement curious. He and Isaac were quasi-superintendents. Handled trash, shoveled snow, showed units to prospective tenants in their building and other properties Mrs. Sheridan, the landlady, owned.

"What's the gig?" she asked.

Property management, he said. He was still showing Mrs. Sheridan's units. Painting them too. And he was getting his real estate license. "It's crazy out here, the money from flipping houses. Mrs. Sheridan's been cleaning up."

That's her main thing now? Nina wondered. Houses? Nina knew her as the wig lady. She owned one of the biggest wig and beauty supply stores in Roxbury and another on Central Avenue in Cambridge.

Of course, Devon didn't need a license to flip houses. But she told him it certainly wouldn't hurt to have one in addition to his degree.

"Exactly."

"Listen, I'm trying to catch up with Isaac."

"He was gone when I got up."

Nina didn't want to assume what Devon knew about Isaac's legal difficulties so she didn't mention the attorney. "When are you coming by so we can really catch up?"

Sunday's were usually good, he told her, though not today.

"Next Sunday work for you?" she asked. "Around 6?"

He said he'd be there.

Nina Sojo had first seen Devon Mack in a second-grade St. Louis classroom. She was the sub. He began the day beating on the kid beside him—any kid beside him. And the boy roamed. She tried to manage him by keeping him on task with challenging puzzles, painting, and storybooks. But there were twenty-three other kids with matching proclivities. Before noon, he had kicked the trash can at Nina's bent back. She'd spun around, dropped the loaded can on the boy's head, and made the terror clean the mess that rained down over him. "And don't you ever in your life even think of kicking me, or anything at me, again." Later, she took him aside and said that when little boys are so ready to fight it usually means they are unhappy about something. "Are you unhappy about something?" By 3:15 he was slumped in her arms, his eyes overrun ponds. *Will you come back tomorrow? Are you ever coming back? Why can't you come back?* The questions of too many sad children she'd meet year after year.

Nina had discovered his birthday was the following week and showed up that day with a cake, coloring books, and a box of Crayolas in a big red bag. The principal arranged for Nina to drive Devon home.

"Where you taking me?" the boy demanded, cringing in the backseat of her car.

"Your house. They know we're coming."

Four blocks later, Nina encountered a pregnant teenager and an older woman waiting with smiles. And Devon's hard jaw relaxed.

Nina sent the boy a card every birthday for three years. Then stopped for four. Nothing matched the way she felt those years. Then, early in '98, Devon's sister—the pregnant girl—sent Nina an e-mail. Her AOL address had been printed on the business card Nina planted in the big red bag. Tania Mack said her health wasn't too good and asked, *Could you check on my baby brother time to time?* He still lived with their aunt, but the aunt's new husband wouldn't mind seeing Devon gone. Tania died of leukemia shortly after that and Devon went to stay with Isaac. They were already living in the Roxbury sweet spot when Nina arrived.

She called their Fort Hill place sweet because of the area's history and the quality of the renovated housing. The Hill had been known for its tie-dye-and-dashiki brigades when she was at Berklee. The dissidents and artists remained, renovated and spurred investment from people like Mrs. Sheridan. Isaac and Devon's unit had elegant crown moldings, granite counters, a spa tub . . . in exchange for shoveling snow. And use of Sheridan's company vehicle: a 2001 black Durango. Nina wanted their gig.

Before taking Devon in, Isaac had been rooming with another student in a nice-looking space around the corner from Dorchester's "Hell Zone." Murder round the clock. After sundown, thugs ran the streets while owners of homes worth a half-million cowered in their parlors.

Tania and her baby-daddy had had an understanding.

He'd made the hookup that put Devon and Isaac in the sweet spot. "He's friends with Mrs. Sheridan. Both of them are Korean," Isaac eventually explained, one long weekend months ago.

"Korean immigrants, you mean?"

"Uh-uh. Korean American." The man had big money and a big family, Isaac went on, holding Nina close. They were cuddlers big-time, for about four weeks.

"You know him?" Nina had asked.

"I know he had a thing for Tania."

Tania couldn't have been more than sixteen when Nina met her. She'd asked about Tania's baby and learned it had been put up for adoption. All of it arranged before the child was born.

These days, Nina was still suspicious of the living arrangement. She didn't tell Isaac, but she had met the landlady.

Mrs. Sheridan tagged her late husband's name to her real estate enterprise and *Paradise* to her beauty supply business.

Nina had been to the Paradise location in Roxbury. It was a long space, with three aisles. She'd barely been inside a minute when a stocky Latino guy coming one way fingered the crotch of a voluptuous Jamaican sister walking opposite him down the middle aisle. The woman wore black leggings and a smile. She tried to swivel around him while he held on a few more seconds. Evidently, the maneuver helped an itch get scratched. They both worked there. He custom-blended hair for weaves and braids. The woman cut and styled wigs. She had a busy operation. Two in chairs, four waiting. Her partner, built like a sprinter, cut hair like one too. Fast. Nina liked the way she was layering the cut on one customer's wig. They called the sprinter *Rocket*, Nina would learn later. And it had nothing to do with speed.

Juliette Choo Sheridan, the owner, clearly spent some time in the mirror. It reflected pinkish-red hair swept into a short, spiky ponytail. Blunt cut bangs that stopped short of her carefully placed false lashes—just a few spidery ones on the upper lids. And pouty pink lips. Between all that and the red boots with stiletto heels was a tight black dress to tone things down. Nina had eyed the plunging V-neck for signs of wrinkles. But Mrs. Sheridan didn't have enough tits for cleavage. Nina figured she was forty-three.

"You should try this," Mrs. Sheridan had suggested, pointing to a golden-hued version of the short dark wig Nina held.

Nina had smiled. "I don't think so."

"Ohhhh, you too conservative," Mrs. Sheridan scolded, scanning Nina's bare face. "You pretty lady. Don't be afraid to jazz it up."

Nina was standing in Bruno Magli pumps and wearing an Italian blue tweed suit worth several grand. The suit's short skirt proved one reason Tina Turner had hired her.

When Nina responded, "I'll bear that in mind," the temperature in that zip code dropped ten degrees.

Nina fell asleep after talking to Devon. It couldn't have been a deep sleep; her armpits woke her up. Or maybe it *was* deep and she was just one frowsy bitch. She hadn't showered and the stink enveloped her.

Suitably deodorized, she put on a T-shirt and yoga pants. Ate some yogurt and a banana. And turned on Betty Carter.

Nina checked her e-mail while Betty sang "Spring Can Really Hang You Up the Most."

Isaac had sent a thank-you message. He and the lawyer connected. *I'm seeing her Monday. I'll let you know what happens.*

* * *

He did. The lawyer wanted cash up front, he explained in his next e-mail. He was a student. *She said I was a little boy.*

On Tuesday, Isaac's case was continued. Nina considered this her cue to wish him *Godspeed.* Heading over to the Newton courthouse had entered her mind. Get a peek at the Collar. Check out the public record. Read the complaint. But she was saved from herself when a Berklee prof and his wife invited her to Martha's Vineyard for a week. She rearranged her schedule and left Thursday.

From the ferry ride over to her last breakfast at The Grind, Nina continually ran into characters from her life's first act. Most significantly Barry. Her stabbing victim.

They stared.

He did a playful bob-and-weave. "Do I dare come closer?" he asked.

Why not? It was only a superficial wound. He had easily disarmed her.

He had been a player. Did time for a mob-related shooting in the '60s. Fresh out of Norfolk State Prison, he had cruised Boston with Nina in a spanking new '78 Corvette one week, a '77 Peugeot the next. Both cars compliments of the unofficial wives Nina knew nothing about. Barry was a decent bass guitarist and, these days, a vocational counselor.

It was late morning in Martha's Vineyard. They sat outside an Edgartown café. He remembered how she drank tea instead of coffee.

"You crossed my mind the other day," Nina told him.

"Why? Caught a foul smell or something?"

"I needed the name of a decent criminal attorney."

"I don't know any in Boston worth a dime," Barry charged.

She told him why she had been tempted to call and gave the case CliffsNotes.

Barry's lightning assessment: "This dude sounds like a jive turkey to me." Then he told her—two types of guys volunteer to talk to cops: the ones who really are stupid, and the ones who think that they're smarter than everyone else.

Isaac got a new lawyer. Juliette Choo Sheridan paid. The Collar asked for several more continuances. Too many and a case can get dismissed. But these gave Isaac more time to fuck up.

Late September, he and Devon came home to their Fort Hill sweet spot and couldn't get in: locks changed. Later that night, while crashing with friends: Durango reclaimed. Juliette Choo Sheridan owned the property and knew where the tapes had been buried.

The money shot: Isaac yanking the leash on a bitch blowing his cock. Devon's plugging her ass. The leash was black leather and thin; the collar rhinestone-studded and delicate. Nina cataloged the scene as S&M Lite, but still unbecoming a former Marine and M.I.T. scholar—especially one facing an assault charge and looking for a university gig. The action around Isaac was more damning. Rocket from Paradise—her tits were like missiles—was one of two women being gang-raped. For insurance, the video was all over the Internet before Juliette Choo Sheridan sent copies of it to the prosecutor and the Collar's home address. She and Sindi, former rivals, had become comrades.

Isaac took Mrs. Sheridan's money, fucked to her satisfaction, but refused to move into her Newton contemporary mansion—which Sindi had frequently cased. And Sheridan joining an African harem had never been an option.

* * *

Early in December, Isaac's attorney—he was back to the Roxbury sister—got a plea agreement. There was evidence of guilt but no hard proof. He could apply for a job and truthfully say he'd never been convicted of a crime.

By January, Devon was back in St. Louis and Isaac Elimu Sayif, a.k.a. Calvin Isaac Nethersole, a.k.a. Lite Dick Nethersole (most popular on the Internet), had unwanted websites sprouting like fungi after rain. The sexploits of Lite Dick streamed against the hazy image of his curriculum vitae and generated 87,000 hits on the worldwide web every day, 609,000 each week, 2,436,000 each month . . .

Isaac remains all but dissertation six years later.

TURN SPEED

BY Russ Aborn

North Quincy

At the close of his twenty-third birthday, Michael Mosely sat behind the wheel of a 1968 Chevy Bel Air, looked around the empty bank parking lot, lifted a pint of vodka, and took a good slug. He screwed the top on and put it under the passenger seat. He sat up straight, shook his head like a dog drying off, pulled the shift lever on the column toward him, dropped it into drive, and eased the nose of the car out onto Broadway. Amped and fuzzy at the same time, he cranked the window down to let in the clammy night. The windshield wipers squeaked into action, smearing greasy mist into greasy streaks. He looked to the left, and cut the wheel hard right, making the power steering squeal and moan. He toed the gas. The right rear tire dropped off the curbstone, thumping into the gutter with a hollow, rubbery sound.

He inched along beside the high curb, rolled by the bank, and braked to a quiet stop in front of the steak house. Using his left hand, he pinched the fleshy web on his right hand. The pain yanked him back to his body and sharpened his mind.

A swirl of darkness exploded through the glass front doors of the steak house, and three men wearing Red Sox caps atop blurry faces rushed at the car. Two of the men held handguns, while the man in the middle clutched a satchel like it was Ann Margaret.

TJ, carrying the bag, yanked the front passenger door open and jumped in. Paul pulled the back door open and dove in headfirst, followed by Larry, large and loud. He slammed the door closed and yelled.

"Go!"

The air in the car boiled with kinetic energy, but the scenery outside didn't change.

"Nope," Michael said. "Not until you say please."

The large man tried to articulate some sort of threat, but only produced a lowing noise.

The thin guy sitting shotgun looked sad but sounded giddy. "Oh no. That's not funny, man."

"Time, little brother," the guy directly behind Michael said. He put his hand on Michael's shoulder. "Gotta go. Not too fast. Slick road." Michael looked at his brother Paul in the rearview mirror, then stomped on the gas, pinning them all to their seats. The five-year-old green sedan, as anonymous as a telephone pole, zipped down Broadway toward Sullivan Square.

"Okay, ladies," Paul said, "get down so we can take off the stockings."

In shotgun, TJ pulled off the stocking mask as he slid out of his seat and into the foot well like liquid mercury.

"TJ," Michael said, "be a good fella and hand me my jug while you're down there."

"No, you can wait, Mikey," Paul answered from the floor in the back.

"Just need to loosen the straps a little," Michael said.

"Fuck! Stop fuckin' talkin'!" Larry was the size of a newborn killer whale, and now wedged in between the seats, he sounded near hysteria. "You're s'posed to be alone if anyone fuckin' sees you, you stupid fuckin' fuck. Just drive the fuckin' car, you fuck. Fuck the fuckin' booze."

"Aunt Betty'd slap your face," Michael said, "if she knew how her little Larry swore—"

"Shut up about my mother!" Larry barked.

"Easy, boys. Mikey, anyone behind us?"

Michael checked the rearview. "Just the dark."

At the Sullivan Square traffic circle Michael spun the car around the far edge, with the tires slipping, and then whipped up the crumbling street that ran along the short section of elevated road. A quarter-mile up, the car turned right at Middlesex Avenue and then broke off a fast right into the employee parking lot at the First National Stores grocery warehouse, where there must have been three hundred cars parked in the open dirt lot.

Michael slipped the Chevy Bel Air down to the row of cars against the chain-link fence and stopped at a dark '65 Ford Falcon. The three passengers got out. Paul keyed open the trunk of the Falcon, and they tossed in their guns, hats, stockings, and the money bag. TJ pulled off his sweatshirt, dropped it in the Falcon's trunk, and pulled out two license plates and a screwdriver. He moved to the front of the Chevy Bel Air, ducked out of sight, and popped up again before Michael had time to find his Zippo, chunk it open, and fire up his Winston. TJ paused at Michael's window on his way to the back of the Chevy with the second license plate.

"That's it for me," TJ said. He was wearing an Esso gas station T-shirt with the name *Thomas* over the pocket. "You suck to work with. I'm not going back to jail." Thomas Jefferson Moran walked to the back of the Chevy.

Paul knocked on the passenger window, and Michael leaned over and rolled it down.

"What's TJ saying?" Paul asked. He leaned in the passenger side as he pulled off his warm-up pants. Underneath a bulky turtleneck sweater he wore a white shirt and a red silk tie.

"Nothing, post-game jitters. You're all dolled up."

"Late date." Paul turned back and closed the trunk of the Falcon. He threw the trunk key over the fence, out into the growth of bulrushes in the marsh.

Larry got into the front passenger seat of the Chevy. He had worn a Patriots jersey during the robbery, now he had on a Led Zeppelin T-shirt.

"Rock on, man!" Michael said. He held his hand up for a high five.

Larry sneered. "One of these days, Michael."

Paul and TJ got back in the Chevy and Michael dropped each of the three at their own cars, which they had driven to the lot earlier that night.

Michael parked the Chevy, fished the vodka out, and took a drink. He got a rag from his back pocket, soaked it with vodka, and wiped down all the surfaces in the car that anyone might have touched. Then he tossed the Chevy key over the fence. He drank the last of the vodka, dropped back, and tried to spiral the bottle over, hoping to reach the oily creek, but it fell short and smashed into something solid, silencing the marsh.

He walked up two rows to his car, a black GTO. He put his key in the door, and felt the top end of his throat stretch itself wide. He turned his head and threw up beside the car. Wiping his mouth with the rag, he muttered, "Fuckin' egg salad."

He placed his feet carefully around the puddle, opened the door, and dropped backwards onto the driver's seat, pulling his feet in.

When he was done shaking, he woke the Goat and drove it to North Quincy.

* * *

The Sagamore Grill was the name on the liquor license, but it was commonly known as The Sag, partly because there was no actual grill. The only grill any of the patrons ever saw was the cross-worked iron bars at the Quincy police station.

On Saturday morning, Michael sidled up and placed his order with Bud, the day bartender. "Hi, neighbor, I'll have a 'Gansett, please."

Larry and TJ came in together, stopped at the far end, and ordered. Bud lifted the hose from behind the bar and squirted soda into a couple of glasses. They crossed the room to sit at a red square Formica table, way at the back. Michael took his beer and followed.

"Look at this guy," Larry said to TJ. "Beer for breakfast. My aunt's dying of cancer and her son's getting gassed every time I see him."

"When you're not here, I drink milk," Michael said. "I see you, I lose the will to live."

The front door opened and Paul came in followed by the sun, and by the time the door chopped off the outside light, he was cutting a path through the tables. Michael watched him move; fast, without hurrying; covering a lot of ground with deceptive speed. Paul sat down at the small table.

"Hey," Michael said. "I forgot to ask, how was your date last Saturday?"

"Good. Nice girl, but not the one. The search continues," Paul replied.

"Girl from work?" Larry asked.

"In a way. I met her when I took a customer to lunch. She was our waitress."

Paul was a sales rep for Triple-T Trucking, a union carrier that operated in the New England and the metro New York–New Jersey area.

"Which customer?" Michael asked. He was a driver for Triple-T, jockeying trailers around, making local deliveries and pickups.

"The traffic manager from Schrafft's Candy, he suggested this place, which, I found out too late, doesn't take credit cards. I didn't want to look like a chump, so when the check came, I pretended to go to the restroom, flagged down the waitress, said I didn't have enough cash on me. I was short a buck for the bill and had no money for a tip. I told her if she lent me a dollar and waited for the tip, it would be a good one. I went back the next day, gave her a fifty, and asked her out for Saturday. She said she was working; I said after. I'd be in the area."

Michael watched Larry and TJ do the quick nod, polite but impatient, waiting for Paul to get to the good part: their share of the robbery. Michael took a drink from his beer, brought the bottle down, and rapped the bottom against the tabletop a few times.

"Get it?" Michael said. Larry and TJ stopped nodding and looked over at him.

"Cash only," Michael said. "No cards? That was our restaurant last Saturday night."

Larry's jaw fell like the trapdoor on a gallows. TJ shook his head.

"And you went back to pick up the girl?" Larry asked.

"Shhh. Turn it down," Paul said. He leaned back against the booth in his bright white starched shirt. No matter how grimy the environment, somehow Paul remained spotless.

"Did you know?" TJ asked Michael.

"I just figured it out," Michael said. "Anyway, how *did* we do?"

Paul shrugged. "Better than we'd do tonight, now that

they're going to start taking credit cards. That's what they get for trying to shortchange the IRS." He flashed a phony smile, followed by a real one; he was charmed by his own insincerity.

"My brother, the patriot," Michael said.

"You get eighteen hundred each," Paul said.

"You get twenty-four," TJ said.

"That's the deal. Twenty-five percent more," Paul said.

"That's thirty-three, isn't it?" Michael asked.

"Okay," Paul said. "Then you get seventy-five percent of what I get, which is twenty-five percent less. Whatever makes you feel better. Either way, it's like five weeks take-home driving a truck."

"What do we do next, boss?" Larry asked.

"Keep in mind," TJ interrupted, "I'm gone. Mahla wants to move to Florida. She don't like the snow."

"What snow? It's June," Michael said.

"Fuck off, man. It gonna stay June?"

The front door opened and they watched a figure lurch into the shadows before TJ spoke again.

"No, I hear you," Paul said to TJ. "Especially with the toy guns. But this new thing has no need for weapons, real or otherwise, which I knew you'd like. We're going to liberate a truckload of cigarettes." Paul smiled like a dust bowl Bible salesman, going face to face to share his look of joy and wonder.

"Cigarettes? From where?" Michael asked.

"One of the car loaders, Blue Ribbon Distributors."

"What's a car loader?" Larry asked.

"A warehouse with a railroad siding. It transfers freight between rail cars and trucks."

"Can't be from Triple-T. We don't haul smokes, or booze either," Michael said.

"We do now. My new boss, Guy Salezzi, is the nephew-in-law of Mr. T.T. Tortello, so I guess he can change the policy. They're going to start using us on cigarette loads to the BPM warehouse in East Bridgewater next week. I've called on Tony Bentini in the Blue Ribbon traffic office for fourteen months and never got a sniff of the work. Why? Because company policy is we won't take cigarettes, and he won't give me any other loads unless we take them too. Nobody wants the smokes. But Salezzi went to Fordham with Bentini. So now we're getting business because they're pals. They're going to give us one load, see if BPM is okay with us. If so, we'll get more."

Larry smiled at his older cousin. "You got some balls, man. You want to knuckle a load the first week?"

"We better act while we can, right? What if we lose the account?"

Michael said, "I guess we're going to ignore the fact—"

"The rumor," Paul cut in.

"—that Mr. T.T. Tortello is a member of the Gambino family."

"Tortello started that rumor so no one would steal from him," Paul said. "This is good for forty grand. Split evenly. We each put ten in our poke." Paul leaned toward TJ. "Think: forty thousand bucks. A few like that and we quit. Become homeowners, family men, good citizens."

"God bless America," Michael said.

"I spent six months at the farm," TJ said. "Watching corn and punkins come up out of the ground. I'm not going back. How long you think you can steal from your company before they start investigating and whatnot?"

"They'll look at the Teamsters," Paul said. "I'm management."

They stared at Michael the Teamster. He snapped open

his Zippo, touched the Winston to the flame, and inhaled. Then he smiled around the cigarette and clapped the lighter closed.

"Is Michael going to get this load?" TJ asked.

"No, they pick up at 3 p.m.," Paul replied. "He starts at 6 a.m. He's on OT at 3. They'd give the pickup to a straight time guy. We have fifty drivers that start at 8."

"Good chance I'll deliver it, though," Michael said. "There's only two of us at 6."

Paul nodded. "BPM wants all loads backed in and ready to unload when their crew starts at 7 a.m. Which means the driver will come from the 6 start." He looked at his brother. "If Rosie gives you the P&G or the Jordan Marsh load, you call the apartment, let the phone ring once, and hang up. If you get the right load, *don't* call. Even Rosie might notice if you did. If you don't get this one, we'll have to hope you get the next, assuming there is a next."

"And listen, Michael," Larry warned, "lay off the booze! Someone might smell you."

Paul turned to Michael and raised his eyebrows but didn't look directly at him. "He makes a good point, Mikey. Work has to come first. By the way, go see Ma today, will you? Eat something, take a nap, and go see her."

Michael pulled the GTO up behind the old man's Rambler, across the street from the house, a small brown bungalow with a screened porch. A strip of sidewalk and a patch of grass separated the house from the street. If an eighteen-year-old kid who stood six feet tall tripped in the gutter and fell forward, his head would bounce off the bottom cement step. The morning after the night that Michael proved that, his father had thrown him out.

Paul leaned against the kitchen sink holding a glass of water, while their father sat in his chair at the same spot at the same table they'd had since Michael was a small boy.

"Here he is, Dad," Paul said. "I'll go slay the fatted calf."

"Michael. How've you been?" His father stood and offered his hand.

"Hey, Dad." They shook. "You say that like you haven't seen me in years. I was here, what, two weeks ago?"

"Yeah? Seems longer."

"How's Ma?"

"Go up and see. She's awake, we just put her in the chair."

Upstairs in the front bedroom, their mother was propped up in her wheelchair looking out at the street. While on chemo for breast cancer, she had a stroke, or a *shock*, as his aunts called it. Her left hand had curled into a claw, and her whole left arm was as rigid as the left side of her face was slack.

"Hi, Ma." He kissed her forehead and put his chin on the top of her head. His eyes stung, and he squeezed the bridge of his nose until it hurt enough to stop the tears. He kissed her cheek and sat at the foot of the bed, hunched forward, his elbows on his knees, as they both peered out the window.

"Michael?" Her voice sounded like she'd swallowed shards of glass, and the way she said his name broke his heart. "When will it stop?"

Michael stared down at his feet. "Pretty soon, Ma."

It was a warm day and the windows were up as life passed by on the street below. Kids on Sting-Ray bikes with towels draped around their necks hollered at each other on their way to Wollaston Beach; young mothers pushed strollers carrying big-headed toddlers; cars rolled by, windows down, volume up, sharing the thump with one and all, like it or not.

It was hard for Ma to speak, but his three sisters were here every day, and their kids visited several times a week, so she had more family news than he did. The result was Michael stretched out sideways on the bed with his hands folded on his stomach, talking to her about his softball team, which was just fine. What he said didn't matter, she just needed the comfort of his voice.

He heard the steps squeak and a few seconds later his father came into the bedroom. He sat in an armchair and they talked about Yaz and the Red Sox. If Michael wanted to avoid the AA jive he had to stay on his toes. When the conversation began to slow, he moved rapidly to other safe topics, like politics, war, and religion. Yet the old man could spot the smallest opening and race through it, turning an innocent remark about the weather into a tale of winos in winter. Many were the trolls pulled from under a bridge and into a meeting by a hazy memory of free donuts—but not all who were called by the pastry were chosen by the higher power to live clean, dry lives, and those who were gave thanks to the program, the program, the program.

His mother was snoring softly in her chair. She'd sleep on and off until late evening. Most nights she'd lie awake in the dark, listening to Larry Glick on the radio.

"She's been asking me if I think you're going to stop soon," his father said.

"Yeah, I'll stop by again soon." Michael looked at his watch and stood up. "Now I gotta scoot. I'll be back in the next few days, okay?"

"Yeah," his foiled father said, a note of resignation in his voice. "Okay."

Paul was still downstairs and he walked out with his brother.

"Did you ever deliver to Pat's Vending down in Providence?" Paul asked.

Michael looked up to his mother's window as they walked across the street to his car. "A number of times. New candy and tonic machines, mostly."

"They own a ton of cigarette machines too, in bars and strip joints. The owner's son is going to take the Blue Ribbon load. He'll get top dollar in the machines."

"This won't do your new boss Salezzi any good, will it?"

"Probably not." Paul smiled and shrugged. "It's a tough game."

At 6 a.m. on Wednesday, Rosie the dispatcher handed Michael the BPM delivery papers. "You get our first load from this shipper, Mosely. Try not to screw it up."

Michael walked out of the terminal into the truck yard and climbed up into his tractor, a spotless red U-model Mack. He turned the key to the on position and pushed in the black rubber nipple on the dash, kicking the diesel to life. At the top of the long sideview mirror he saw dull gray smoke roll out of the stack. He fed the noisy beast some fuel, and the smoke, now thinned by heat, shot out of the pipe. He pushed in the clutch, wiggled the stick into second, and, with the heel of his hand, whacked the pentagonal red button on the dash. With a sharp *whoosh*, the tractor brake was off and so was he, over to the trailer pad, searching for the right trailer, number 5432. There were five rows of trailers, about a hundred in all, but the high-value load would be in the first row. He found it, turned the truck away from it, and stopped fast, skidding the eight tires on the rear axles. He looked at the three mirrors while he wiggled the stick into reverse, took a bead on the trailer, and rushed the tractor backwards at the box. He stopped when the fifth wheel was about an inch from the bottom of the trailer. He pulled out the red pentagon to lock the air brake, slipped the vehicle into neutral, opened the door, and swung himself out.

Standing on the grate at the back of the tractor, between the tractor and trailer, he unhooked the hoses for the trailer brakes and the light cord that hung on the back of the Mack, then coupled them with the connections on the trailer, swung back into the cab, popped it in reverse, and rammed the fifth wheel under the trailer. The box lifted as the Mack wedged underneath, the kingpin locked, and Michael put the stick in first gear, left the trailer brake on, and tried to pull back out from beneath the box. He rocked the coupled unit violently, trying to break the grip. The last thing he wanted was to make a turn out on the road and see the trailer uncouple and go zipping off alone. The trailer felt light, but he was used to pulling loads out of P&G; a full load of soap could weigh forty-two thousand pounds.

He switched on the lights and flashers and got out to do a series of visual checks, along with bopping the tires with a mallet, checking for flats. At the back of the trailer, he checked the security seal on the doors. To open the doors, the skinny metal strip had to be cut. It was stamped with a unique number that had already been called in to BPM security. The guard at BPM was supposed to come out to verify the seal number, but he wouldn't have to today.

Michael walked toward the front of the box and rolled up the landing gear. He climbed into the Mack, slammed the stick into second, and punched the brake buttons. The brakes released with a great hiss, then he popped the clutch and the tractor roared and jumped ahead, slamming the driver's door closed with a metallic bang, as the trailer slid out of its hole.

He was in fourth gear by the time he swept around the corner of the building. At the far end of the yard the security gate was closed. He aimed at it, building speed and pulling on the air horn cord, and the gate seemed to jump before it rolled aside.

Thirty minutes later, Michael was stopped at a red light on Route 106. A hand reached in the open passenger window, pulled up the lock button, and TJ climbed in.

"There's no seat here." TJ crouched, like someone would be right along to bolt a seat to the floor underneath him.

"Close the door and sit on the floor. Get down, will ya!"

"People are supposed to see me so you can say you were hijacked."

Michael had no answer to that, so he just glared straight ahead. The light turned green, the truck lurched, and the matter was resolved by TJ falling on his ass.

At Route 18, they headed south.

TJ stretched to see the sideview mirror. "Is Larry still behind us in the van?"

"Silly bastard is so close I can't even see him," Michael said. "It's like he's skid-hopping me."

"Boy, you're a real grouch. Is it because you're hungover? Or not drinking?"

At the Middleboro Rotary they picked up Route 44 west and had the road almost to themselves.

"That the sign?" Michael took his foot off the accelerator.

"That's it," TJ affirmed. "Weir Brothers Saw Mill."

Michael checked his mirrors, braked, then geared down the transmission and pressed the fuel pedal, swinging into the turn.

"Man, you took that fast. It's a miracle you didn't tip this over."

"We were going too fast to slow down. You go into a turn on the brake and you wreck."

They bumped along a wide asphalt road until it became a single-lane cement dust strip. At the end, in the middle of an enormous hangar wall, was a rusted corrugated sliding door, twenty feet high, forty feet wide.

"We're supposed to drive right in."

"I vote we open the door first," Michael said. He rolled the truck up near the door and stopped.

"Paul said we should drive right in."

"He may have assumed that between us we'd figure out what to do if the door was closed. I think we should try to open it first. I can always crash the truck through it, you know, if nothing else works."

Thomas Jefferson Moran jumped out like a parachutist, landed, and walked toward the door, turning a 360 as he went, glancing in all directions. He grabbed the handle on the metal door with his right hand, leaned all the way to the left, using his weight to slide the door open. He almost fell when the door rolled easily. He turned and gave his accomplice the finger.

Michael put on his headlights to see a wide cement floor inside the hangar. He played the clutch out, and the truck crept inside, TJ walking along beside it. Michael hit the high beams and about a hundred yards off, at the back of the hangar, he could make out piles of unfinished picnic tables. He swung the steering wheel left and right, using the tractor like a giant flashlight, looking for the empty rental trailer that was supposed to have been left inside. Back in the van, Larry had lengths of metal rollers they were going to use to convey the freight from the Triple-T trailer to the rental box. But all Michael saw in front of him was the inside of a cavernous, abandoned saw mill.

Larry pulled the van inside the building, up near the front of the trailer. He stopped and was getting out when Michael jumped down from the tractor.

"Where's the empty trailer?" Larry asked. "They were supposed to leave it by last night at the latest. What's the story?"

"How would I know?" Michael answered.

"Should we just leave this trailer here?" TJ said. "Should we unload it?"

"I don't know," Michael snapped. He walked back to the trailer doors, took out a jackknife, and sawed at the seal until it broke. He opened the doors carefully in case the load had shifted. There was always a chance something could fall out and land on your head. But not today; the trailer looked almost empty, other than some cartons he could see in the nose. "Aw, shit." Michael climbed in the trailer and walked up to the nose. When he returned, he went to the back end of the trailer and looked up at the number stenciled in black at the top inside corner. "Forty-five seventy?" he said.

He jumped down, grabbed the trailer door, pushed it closed, and stared at the four-digit number affixed to the door: 5432. He pulled at the corner of the number on the outside of the trailer door, peeled the decal off, and revealed a different number underneath: 4570.

"He put phony numbers on."

"Who?" TJ asked. "How?"

"How's easy. There're cartons full of number decals in the repair shop." Michael looked at his watch. "Let's go. Quick." He gestured to Larry. "Give me the van keys."

Michael drove the van, Larry rode shotgun, and TJ sat on the floor between the seats.

"What was up in the front?" Larry asked.

"Eight pallets of Cocoa Puffs."

Michael pulled the van into one of the spaces in the drivers'
parking lot at Triple-T Trucking.

"You gotta say something, man," Larry mumbled. "What
are we doing here?"

Michael looked at his watch. "Good. Five of 8."

"So," TJ said, "are we surrendering or what? You got a
plan?"

Michael pointed toward the terminal building, a mon-
strosity the length of three football fields that had dock doors
numbered 60 through 140 on the side facing them.

"See the ramp? And all those red Macks parked in rows?
At 8, it's going to look like a jail break. About fifty guys are
going to come down that ramp, jump in those tractors, and
start driving around, all over the yard. Some will hook up to
trailers backed into the dock doors, the rest are headed to the
trailer pad in the back to hook up out there. I'm going to go
in the repair shop and get a dupe key from the cabinet. Jimmy,
the Waltham driver, is on vacation this week and nobody will
use his tractor. He eats his lunch in it and throws the bags on
the floor. It smells like a restaurant dumpster."

"Why? What are you doing?" Larry asked. "Why don't we
call Paul?"

"On what? You and him got shoe phones?"

"On a pay phone," Larry said.

"Okay. Where is he? Where do I call?"

"I don't get what we're doing," TJ said.

"These guys don't screw around. If we want to keep
breathing, we need those cigarettes."

"What cigarettes? That's my answer," TJ said. "We don't
have none. Never did."

"Which guys? Who we're stealing from? Or selling to?" Larry asked.

"Both, probably," Michael speculated.

"I *knew* this was a bad idea," TJ said. "My grandmother was right. First time I got pinched, she said, 'Thomas, be careful. Life's going to be tricky for you because you're a complete fuckin' idiot.' I said, 'Me? No way.' She had me pegged."

"Why do you think the load is here?" Larry asked.

"What's a better place to hide a forty-five-foot Triple-T trailer?" Michael said. "They're on 4570. Not the real one, but one here with that number on it. Look, you want to, go home, I'll keep you guys out of it."

"Screw you," Larry said. "We stick together."

Larry looked at TJ, who closed his eyes and nodded. "It's what we do."

The receiving department for Pat's Vending was around the back on a side street. Although cars were parked on both sides of the road, there were *No Parking* signs posted near the receiving doors so Michael had plenty of room to draw the trailer up along the curb. He pulled out the plunger on the dash and the engine shuddered and died. He turned the key off and jumped out.

The dock doors on the building were pulled down and a sign read, *No Deliveries After 11 a.m.*

At the top of the cement steps there was an employee entrance door. Michael pressed a black button inside a brass ring and a shrill bell sounded. He backed down a couple of steps just before the door flew open. There stood a tall, young man. Michael had delivered here many times, and this receiver, Victor, always acted as if he'd never seen him before. Victor sported his usual Sha Na Na get-up: starched white T-shirt, new jeans, and an elaborate hairdo.

"What?"

"I've got a delivery."

"Can you read?" Victor jerked a thumb in the direction of the roll-up door and the *No Deliveries* sign.

"I sure can. Let me help you out." Michael squinted at the sign and moved his lips. "It says, *No Smoking*. Okay now, Bowzer, you do me a favor. Go tell Junior I have his delivery."

Victor shifted his weight to his left foot, reached up to grab the doorjamb with his left hand, and stretched his right out to grab the other jamb. Michael closed the distance between them and, using both hands, grabbed Victor high on his arms and pressed his thumbs into the nerves on the inside of Victor's biceps. Michael pushed him inside the darkened warehouse while Victor emitted a series of high-pitched yips.

"You gonna boot me in the kisser?" Michael said. He grabbed the front of Victor's T-shirt with two hands and twisted it hard to the right, and the man toppled to the side, almost to the floor. Michael held onto him, then lifted him back up and released his shirt. He pretended to smooth out Victor's tee and dust him off.

"Now, Victor," Michael smiled and patted him on the cheek, "go get Junior, or so help me God I'll muss up your swirly hairdo."

He shoved Victor backwards, just as another man came out into the warehouse from the office. This man had a confused and unhappy look on his face. "Hey, what's going on? Who is this guy?"

"I'm Michael Mosely and you're Junior. I have a delivery for you."

"Oh no. No. You didn't bring them here." He ran to the exit door and looked out. "Is that them? Tell me you didn't. Mr. T. is on his way here. We're all dead."

"Give me our money. I'll drop the trailer. You can give it back to Mr. T.," Michael said.

"No!" Junior raised his hands in the surrender pose. "No. I'll give you the hundred I promised your brother, I have the cash, but you gotta screw, with the truck."

"Okay. Get the money."

"No, get out of here and come back later."

"And what, you'll give me a check?" Michael said.

Junior walked over to a tall, gray metal desk against the wall, opened a drawer, and pulled a pistol out. He pointed it at Michael. "Get going. Move."

Michael walked down the steps, over to the tractor, with Junior right behind him. Michael opened the door to the tractor and turned. "Where do you want it?"

"Take off, or I'll shoot you where you stand," Junior said.

"Don't be hasty. I'll get the trailer out of here after I get the money. My pals in the van across the street there have guns pointed right back at you."

Junior kept his weapon on Michael and pivoted around in a half-circle. The back door of the van was open. TJ and Larry were inside on the floor with pistols aimed at Junior.

At that moment, a bright yellow Lincoln Continental came around the corner and rolled to a stop right beside Junior and Michael. The rear window on the driver's side slid down to display a very old man who looked as if he had been poured into the folds of the leather seat. He had an inert, baggy face, and the thin, wispy hair of a newborn.

"Junior, is that my driver you're menacing with a firearm?"

The Lincoln driver's tinted window stayed closed. The engine burbled, and Michael imagined a couple of slicked-down gorillas in the front seat pointing their guns at Larry and TJ.

"We're just kidding around, Mr. Tortello," Junior said. He bent down and looked in the backseat. "I didn't know until late last night these cigarettes were yours. I called Pop to ask him what I should do."

"Your father called me from Atlanta, Junior. He's green-lighted you, if I feel I've been insulted. You weren't trying to insult me by stealing from me, were you?"

"Goodness no, Mr. T." He put his hand on his collarbone and raised his eyes skyward. "I would never."

"Is that my load of cigarettes?"

"Yes sir, it is," Junior said.

"How much money do you have inside?" Mr. T. asked.

"I don't know exactly. Maybe two hundred thousand."

"How much were you going to pay this fella?"

"A hundred. But honestly, Mr. T., I had no idea—"

"A salesman from my company offers you a hot truck and you didn't ask yourself if it could be mine?" Mr. T. shook his head. "Sadly, Junior, I believe you. Do you know why? Because it's a well-known fact you're an imbecile. Your poor father is in prison because you're an imbecile, but why should I do his dirty work? He can kill you himself when he gets out. Go in and get my money, Junior."

"Absolutely. How much should I get?"

"All of it. Take whatever cash your employees have on them too. You can reimburse them later."

"You bet, Mr. T." Junior ran over, vaulted up the cement stairs, and passed by Victor, who was holding the door open.

Mr. T. looked at the driver in the front seat of his car. "Help me get out."

The driver's door opened and a skinny, older blond woman in a chauffeur suit hopped out and opened the back door. She helped Mr. T. peel himself off the seat and pulled him to his feet, then edged him toward her and closed the car door with her knee. She leaned him against the car like a board and fixed his tie. His trousers were pulled up so high that his belt practically bisected his shirt pocket. It didn't look like he was *wearing* a pair of pants, as much as it looked like they were devouring him. The blonde stood at his elbow.

"You're Mosely's brother? Your father worked for us too. The three of you were there when we bought the Boston operation from Blaney," Mr. T. said.

"Yeah, until your terminal manager fired him for poor production. A sixty-two-year-old guy."

"Well, that stinks. But in our defense, he's a drunk, right?" Mr. T. asked.

"He used to be. He's in AA now, so he's an alcoholic."

"Well, your brother never said this was about revenge."

"It is for me," Michael replied.

"I cannot respect suicidal stupidity for purposes of money," Mr. T. said. "But I can for revenge, especially on behalf of a father. Very much so. Tonya, tell Chuck and Brucie to pull the other Mosely out of the trunk."

Michael felt like he'd been bitten by an electric eel.

"Relax. He's fine," Mr. T. said. "He said he didn't know where the load was so he's been manhandled a little. He'll need to be delumped before he goes looking for a new job."

Two very large men got out on the passenger side of the Lincoln, front and rear. Over the roof of the car, Michael saw Larry and TJ get their toy weapons up, as if ready to squirt water at the two goons. Tonya keyed the trunk open and a bloody Paul, bound and gagged, was lifted out. He was conscious and he looked extremely pissed off.

The men set Paul on his feet and one produced a switchblade to cut the rope around his legs and wrists. The other guy peeled the tape off his face. Even the sound of it hurt, but Paul was silent.

"See, Paul," Mr. T. said, "this is why I have a rule. No cigarettes or liquor. They are just too tempting a target for shenanigans."

Paul said nothing, and Larry and TJ came over to help him back to the van. Paul got in, and the other two turned to keep an eye on Chuck and Brucie.

"In case you're wondering," Mr. T. said, "you're fired too."

"Okay, but now I *really* need that hundred thousand. Then I'll go quietly."

"Why would I pay you? We're going to deliver the cigarettes this afternoon," Mr. T. said.

"No, you're not. You'd have called the cops. Instead you switched the numbers so I got the wrong box. You're stealing it too. Your plan was to keep the smokes, file a claim with the insurance company. They'll pay Blue Ribbon for the missing butts."

"You're a shrewd one. When Raymond called last night, I thought this was a chance to make lemonade from lemons. Brucie was going to take the real cigarette trailer out of the yard after the 8 o'clock driver rush was over. But he couldn't find it, so we figured out where Paul was making a sales call and picked him up. But he didn't know anything, so he said. Now Brucie will take this truck down to Jersey. We'll sell the cigarettes there. Cigarettes are way too tempting. But I promised myself I'd just have one."

"Famous last words," Michael said.

"And I'm entitled to collect a fine from Junior. Sounds like it will be about two hundred thousand."

"May I suggest a way to make an additional fifty grand?" Michael asked.

"Please do."

"Keep the tractor and trailer down in Jersey, put new numbers on them, and file a claim for lost equipment."

"You are a smart kid. You'll go far, if someone doesn't kill you first."

"I know it won't be you," Michael said.

"How do you know that?"

"You need me to talk to the insurance company so you can get your claim paid. You don't want to have to pay Blue Ribbon out of your pocket. If I'm found dead right after talking to the FBI and the insurance men, that won't be good."

"I like the cut of your jib, mister."

"Aw shucks," Michael said. "I'm just helping you have a productive day."

"It is a good idea to stay busy at my age," Mr. T. said.

"Yeah? I figured a guy your age would rather be home praying for a peaceful death."

Mr. T. barked two sharp sounds to indicate mirth. "Ha! Ha! I like that."

"So don't I," Michael said.

"That sounds like a Boston thing." Mr. T. turned and looked at his three people. "Wait in the car." He gestured for Michael to come closer. "I feel bad about your father. I'm glad he's off the booze. I'll give you fifty thousand when Junior gets back. Give some to your pop."

When they got back to North Quincy, Larry dropped the brothers at their parents' house. Paul was going to clean up and they were going to borrow the old man's car to get back to the Triple-T parking lot to pick up Michael's GTO.

Michael started up the front stairs with the bag of money for his father under his left arm.

"Hey," Paul said, "my back is sore. Give me a hand going up the stairs."

Michael went back down, and Paul draped his arm over his shoulders. After a moment's thought, Michael handed Paul the bag of cash, reached up and took his brother's left hand in his, then slipped his right arm around Paul's waist and helped him up the stairs.

Their father came out of the house and held open the screen door. "What happened?" he asked.

The brothers made it up to the porch and the door clapped shut behind them.

"It got a little rough," Paul said, "but I got you some money from Tortello." Paul handed the bag to his father and smiled at his brother. "Mikey helped too."

ABOUT THE CONTRIBUTORS

Jen Dolan

RUSS ABORN was born in Boston and lived in Dorchester before the family moved to North Quincy, which he was told was in "the country." He has spent his youth, adulthood, and, most likely, will spend his declining years in the logistics profession. He is married to his high school sweetheart, Susan.

James Goodwin

DANA CAMERON is the author of the Emma Fielding mysteries, including the Anthony Award–winning *Ashes and Bones.* Her short stories, including the Agatha Award–winning "The Night Things Changed," are also set in and around Boston. She has lived and attended university in Boston, and as a professional archaeologist, extensively studied the city's colonial period. She now lives nawtha Boston, but sneaks back in town for the restaurants and museums.

Michael DuBois

BRENDAN DUBOIS is the award-winning, New Hampshire–based author of eleven novels and more than one hundred short stories. His short fiction has earned him two Shamus Awards, three Edgar Award nominations, and inclusion in *The Best American Mystery Stories of the Century,* edited by Tony Hillerman and Otto Penzler. For more information, visit www.BrendanDuBois.com.

Elizabeth Kortlander

JOHN DUFRESNE is the author of two story collections and four novels, the most recent of which is *Requiem, Mass.* His story "The Timing of Unfelt Smiles" appeared in *Miami Noir* and in *The Best American Mystery Stories* (2007). He teaches writing at Florida International University.

Andrei Jackamets

JIM FUSILLI is the author of five novels. In 2008, he was editor of, and contributed a chapter to, *The Chopin Manuscript,* Audible's best-selling "serial thriller," and is editing and contributing a chapter to its sequel, *The Copper Bracelet.* Fusilli is also the rock and pop critic of the *Wall Street Journal. Pet Sounds,* his book on Brian Wilson and the Beach Boys' album of the same name, was published in 2006 by Continuum.

Michael Malyszko

LYNNE HEITMAN worked for fourteen years in the airline industry. She drew on that rich and colorful experience to create the Alex Shanahan thriller series, including *Hard Landing*, which takes place at Boston's Logan Airport, and *Tarmac*, which was named by *Publishers Weekly* as one of the year's best thrillers. Her current titles, *First Class Killing* and *The Pandora Key*, are available from Pocket Books.

Nance Wiatt

DON LEE is the author of two novels, *Wrack & Ruin* and *Country of Origin*, as well as a story collection, *Yellow*. He has received an American Book Award, the Edgar Award for Best First Novel, the Sue Kaufman Prize for First Fiction, an O. Henry Award, a Pushcart Prize, and the Fred R. Brown Literary Award. For nineteen years, he was the principal editor of *Ploughshares*. He now teaches in the graduate creative writing program at Temple University.

Diana Luca

DENNIS LEHANE is the author of eight novels, including *The Given Day, Shutter Island, Mystic River,* and *Gone, Baby, Gone*. Three of his novels have been adapted into major motion pictures, including *Mystic River,* which won two Academy Awards. A native of Dorchester, Massachusetts, Lehane splits his time between the Boston area and West Central Florida.

ITABARI NJERI, winner of an American Book Award and Pulitzer Prize finalist, is author of the memoirs *Every Goodbye Ain't Gone* and *The Last Plantation*. A former reporter for the *Los Angeles Times, Miami Herald,* and Boston Public Radio station WBUR-FM, she attended graduate school at Harvard and holds degrees from Columbia University and Boston University. She currently teaches in Atlanta and is working on her debut novel. "The Collar" is her first published fiction.

Trudy O'Nan

STEWART O'NAN'S story collection *In the Walled City* received the 1993 Drue Heinz Prize. His many novels include *Snow Angels, The Speed Queen, A Prayer for the Dying, Last Night at the Lobster,* and *Songs for the Missing*. With Stephen King, he coauthored *Faithful,* a nonfiction account of the 2004 Red Sox season, and had the pleasure of hanging out around the Fens again, where he used to clean weekly apartments.

Prudence Carter

PATRICIA POWELL was born in Jamaica and emigrated to Boston with her family in 1982. She is the author of *Me Dying Trial, A Small Gathering of Bones, The Pagoda,* and *The Fullness of Everything.* Powell currently lives in California, after spending twenty-five years in Boston. She is a professor of creative writing at Mills College.